The Crystals of Gorn II

Freeing a Slave

TONY PETER

PublishAmerica
Baltimore

First printing

Softcover 9781629079561
PUBLISHED BY PUBLISHAMERICA, LLLP
www.publishamerica.com
Baltimore

Printed in the United States of America

Acknowledgement and Thanks

My wife Betty and my family who support and encourage me to write.

My fellow writers in the Revisionists: they keep me moving and inspire me to write clearer and with more passion and feeling.

Fans that continue asking what happens to the emerald ear stud.

-1-

Only a few weeks before, winter had held an ironclad grip on the land with its endless waves of stark white snowdrifts. However, for the past three days, a warm southerly breeze combined with a strengthening sun produced a definite spring-like mildness. The air swept the face with a warm soothing breath filled with a fresh scent of change. The sharp shape of the snowdrifts rounded as the spring thaw began to take hold. Small pools of water had begun to set up and little rivulets were forming with light murmurs that indicated winter was over.

On days like this, young children enjoy the thrill of splashing through newly formed puddles as well as stomping through the slush. It was still too early for usual enjoyment that comes from the challenge of walking into deep puddles to see if the water will run over the boot tops. Older children find thrills in rolling the sticky snow into various sized balls either for snowmen or for snow forts. Occasionally, smaller snowballs became missiles projected at anyone who happened to be in the vicinity. It is even more interesting and entertaining if the victim is unaware of the impending attack.

Suzy and Timmy walked slowly along the slush-covered road on their way home from school. They were each carrying a school bag in which they had books for homework or study. Both students were very serious about their schoolwork but right now, they were enjoying the foretaste of spring and summer. They gently kicked the snow aside and occasionally stomped into the slush causing it to splash up on each other.

Between their frolicking, Suzy and Timmy found time to contemplate the wonder that they were experiencing and to think about it in the context of their final lessons as they prepared for another major step in their young lives. Spring would mark the time when they would complete their studies for Confirmation; they were about to be asked to take on responsibility for their faith. Timmy and Suzy then would become adult members of their congregation and assume the full rights and duties of membership. These responsibilities weighed heavily on the two of them since they were the only two in their class. They knew and understood the importance of the impending decision.

As they rounded a bend in the road, Timmy and Suzy became aware of a figure standing in the middle of the road. The black dress contrasted starkly with the shiny white surroundings: they knew, without approaching closer, that Emeralda had come for one of her visits. A multitude of memories from their recent trip to Gorn flooded their minds as they recalled their efforts in struggling through the darkness and the freeing of Marlen from the dungeon prison. They recalled how the crystals provided the necessary light to drive out the darkness and then to expel the dark commander. A quick glance between them conveyed the need to be wary, especially for Timmy who hadn't been put to any test by this foe.

Emeralda cackled as they approached. "Little sweet things, so engrossed in your own business. Learning more as if you didn't know enough already. All this is so unnecessary, little princess. You could've had a kingdom and never had to lift a finger or turn a page. It was all yours, but you threw it away. Emeralda was there for you but you had to follow that spiteful old man. You were always so good to that crazy old coot but never showed any concern for poor Emeralda. How many times did I endure suffering and pain, all because no one would come to my aid?"

Suzy shifted her school bag as she looked at the unexpected visitor. "Emeralda, I do feel sorry for you, but not the way you think I should. You could be such a wonderful person, but you always let your greed get in the way."

"Greed…, greed you say, little missy! You're the greedy one. You just couldn't let Emeralda have what's rightfully hers. I guarded that stone and held it when it cried out to me like a baby. I wanted to be a mother to it but when I tried to hold it in my arms, it bit me like some ungrateful brat. The pain of that bite was sheer agony. It rippled through my entire being tearing at my very fabric. In that terrible pain there also was great pleasure, yes, ecstasy, which flowed over my mind and lifted me to great heights. I felt myself floating above the clouds, which moved in obedience to my thought commands. I drifted through an azure sky over fields of splendid flowers, which turned their faces towards me and released the most exquisite fragrances. Terror gripped me and pure delight washed over me. Then darkness descended over me. When I awakened, my baby was gone and I was strapped down, unable to go and find it. Oh, I pleaded for release but my cries stayed within me, as I couldn't move, not even my lips. What pain that was - then the magnificent council of fools who were supposed to be my friends refused to let me have my baby. I could hear it crying out for me but I couldn't respond. My entire system pleaded for another touch from my baby. I needed that so much. I shook, broke into terrible cold sweats, then I was freezing. My flesh, then seemed to be stripped from my bones. Did anyone care? No, no one."

"Snap out of it, Emeralda. Your friends did care and that's why they closely watched you. You'd been terribly injured, nearly destroyed. You couldn't have the lodestone. You weren't strong enough for it. It would've completely destroyed you, if the Sages gave in to your demands." Suzy spoke with authority and determination, yet with a tone of compassion.

"See, I never expected you to understand because that crazy old coot, Marlen, has warped your thinking."

Emeralda turned her attention to Timmy. "Little prince, there's so much in Gorn that you can't possibly understand. You haven't been given the opportunities that you so richly deserve. This one and her cohorts try to prevent you from using your gifts, by keeping you here. I sensed during that first time when we met by the stream that you have a great destiny. I looked into the crystal ball - it revealed a great journey awaits you. I only hope that you're up to it and won't be swayed by those who'd keep you from fulfilling your noble destiny."

"Emeralda, I've heard about you, more than enough." Timmy stepped forward and put up his hand towards Suzy to prevent her from interrupting; he wanted to talk.

"You twist everything, Emeralda. So many people care for you, want the best for you but you don't see it. I don't know you except for the times that our paths crossed - you tried hard to trip me up. I find it hard to believe that you could be so twisted and off-centre yet your sister, Sapphira, is right-minded, gentle, compassionate and duty-bound...."

"Don't you dare bring her into this, you little brat. You don't know anything. You've been so brainwashed that I can't reach you by talking. It's obvious I can't convince you, right now, how much more's available to you if only...." Emeralda turned suddenly and bounded away, rising into the air. A dark crow flew away, cackling hoarsely.

Timmy and Suzy watched as she disappeared from sight. Suzy felt herself trembling. “We have to be careful. She won’t give up.”

“I sense the next time’s going to be more disagreeable.” Timmy kicked some snow.

Without saying any more, Timmy and Suzy parted ways and walked home, deep in thought over what had happened.

-2-

Timmy wandered out to the corral where his father kept the livestock. He had been busy in the house preparing for his Confirmation classes and working on his many homework assignments. He felt the need to get up and have a short rest from the steady pressure of mental activity. At times like this, he liked to walk slowly through the well-wooded yard; often, he made his way to the corrals.

Here his father kept his small herd - Black Angus cattle for meat and for sale, a black and white Holstein cow for milk, and six golden Appaloosas as a hobby and a dear love. His dad carefully groomed and patiently handled these majestic creatures so that they were quiet and accepting of the master's touch. His father trained each of the older five and recently started working with the colt. Right now, however, he was busy else where in the yard, preparing for the inevitable seedtime that would soon arrive.

The older animals were busy grazing on the far side of the corral, pulling out the young tender shoots that had just recently burst through the soil at the call of the spring sun. They raised their golden heads at Timmy's approach, almost as an acknowledgement of his presence and then continued their task. Young Scout kicked up his hooves and went scurrying about the corralled-in area at a fast trot. Here was a spirited animal that showed the bloodlines of his wild ancestors that had roamed the Great Plains of the Western States.

This reminded Timmy of what his father had said one day after he finished working with Scout. "Here's a true champion, a real racer. With the right amount of work this horse could be one of the fastest animals, just mark my words. Maybe one day, the Derby…," and with that his eyes had stared off in the distance as he weaved scenes of a daydream. Timmy's mom had quietly intruded on this flight of imagination with "yes, Harry, I know how much that would mean to you, but don't you think you're being a bit premature. This colt hasn't even been properly broken yet; don't go getting those wild-eyed dreams of yours. I'm sure if it's meant to be, something will happen." Timmy remembered his mother giving his father a tender smile to which he responded in kind and quietly said, "You know, Phyllis, that Scout has something very magical about him and I intend to find out how far he'll go."

Timmy climbed up on the wooden-rail fence that surrounded this portion of the livestock yard. He had a special place for sitting where he could lean against the lamppost that was just outside the fence. Here he could relax and let his mind float off to those faraway places that existed in the minds of every young person.

Today, his thoughts returned to the verses of scripture that he read earlier in preparation for the next Confirmation class. He was studying the life of Daniel and in particular, the tenth chapter in which Daniel had a vision of a messenger that appeared to be an angel. *It's amazing that every time Daniel really needed help or wise counsel, some heavenly being arrived on the scene. I wonder if my life's in tune with what I say I believe or am I like Scout, a wild untrained colt, that races off when startled, pulling against the bridle, resisting the many lessons to be learnt. I think I follow instructions, yet there are times when I catch myself scoffing at some of the lessons.* Timmy knew that his parents really loved and cared for him, but why did he feel they treated him like a child. After all, he was fourteen - he felt that he should have more input in decisions. Timmy ran his hands down his face and peered over his fingers as he watched the colt continue to prance about the yard. *Yes, Scout, you show some very special qualities in your movement. I'm sure you're destined for great things..., so am I.*

Timmy caught himself looking at his hands; he shuddered as he remembered that when these same hands had been placed on some very sick and injured people, their health was restored. *Gosh. I remember the terrible pain and burnt flesh Suzy suffered. My hands healed her, took away her pain. Was that just a dream?*

Timmy recalled meeting Emeralda just the other day on the road - he shuddered at this recollection with its nightmarish side to it. *What does she really want?* He climbed down from his special seat. He looked around and slowly made his way around the corral so that he could be closer to the older horses. The herd of more mature horses consisted of two stallions, a five year old - the sire of the younger two-year old - and three mares, the oldest at six years was the dame of all the younger animals, a three year old and a one year old. Timmy marvelled at the majesty of these fine animals. *I remember the wonder I felt at the sight of this small herd running free across the meadow last year. What a thrill to witness the beauty of these magnificent steeds with their golden manes and tails flowing through the air as they performed their dance of freedom and identity.*

Timmy moved on to where Bessie, the Holstein cow, was relaxing while chewing her cud. Her very round figure gave evidence to the fact that another calf would soon be joining the livestock pen. Bessie was a good cow and came through each delivery with a strong and sturdy calf. Timmy wondered if she would finally drop a heifer - Dad really wanted a successor for Bessie; not that he wanted to replace her, but it was always a good idea to have another cow in the works, just in case. *I hope that this time I can help Dad with the delivery. He hinted that the time was coming for me to be more involved in what goes on around the farm.*

Timmy paused to listen to the chatter of the returning birds - he gazed off into the distance as he heard the faint honking of migrating geese. No doubt, they were using the pond as a resting place. *I should visit that sanctuary as soon as I can. Right now, however, I still have some homework.* The little walk had accomplished its purpose. He turned and started for the house.

-3-

Suzy lay on her stomach on her bed resting on her elbows while flexing her legs back and forth. She gazed at a propped-up book on her pillow but her attention was drifting off. She had been busy reading her bible and trying to grasp the stories of Daniel. This was a Confirmation assignment and she knew that Pastor Adams would be expecting to hear some insights or some questions. These usually led to further discussion and explanation. Right now, she was having difficulty just getting through the book. Some of it just didn't make sense to her and she felt further reading would only confuse the issue more. She wanted to be able to go to her next class with a better understanding of this material; otherwise, it would look as though she hadn't done the required studying. *If only Timmy were here, I know that if the two of us went over the book together, share our thoughts about it, we'd understand this story.*

Strange! We are able to work together so well, finding answers with each sharing in the solution. Suzy remembered from her study of geometric figures that angles that together form a ninety-degree angle were called complements. She wondered if the two of them were complementary, not like angles but in the sense that they were meant to help and support each other. On their trip to Gorn, each had been there for the other so that nothing was accomplished on their own but by the efforts of both. They humbly shared the fame that came their way. *Hmmm! What adventures does the future hold or is it all over? Not likely. After Emeralda's visit the other day, I doubt we've seen the last of her or of Gorn. I wonder how dear old Blog's doing.*

Suzy chuckled how that simple, unassuming bumbler ended up being the leader of a corps of men. Those men came to respect his hidden and unused leadership qualities – his commander was a tyrant who abused his men and didn't allow them to develop any skills. *Aren't we all like Blog in some ways?*

Suzy jumped off her bed and swung around with a flourish, snatching up her Bible and twirling around to her dresser. She carefully placed the book on the top of the dresser and slowly ran her hand along the edge of the top drawer. Then she stared at her hands and quickly removed them from the drawer. The necklace of crystals was inside, hidden under the top of the dresser in her secret compartment. Within it was the little golden chain belonging to Marlen, which held the emerald ear stud that Emeralda had dropped so long ago. Suzy knew she had to be careful because Emeralda desperately wanted it back – her foe could be spying on the house at this very moment. Suzy glanced towards the window and breathed a sigh of relief - the curtains are pulled. *I'd better be more careful from now on. Those gems sure have a way of getting to me.*

Suzy looked at her Bible, remembering the problems that she was having. She ran out the door and down the stairs into the kitchen where her mom was busy kneading the dough she would soon be baking. Her mom glanced her way and smiled.

Suzy blurted out, "I need some help."

Her mom looked up from her task and said with a twinkle of mischief in her eye, "Maybe, you could help with some kneading?"

The two of them giggled.

"Oh, Mom, you know I'm not any good at working with dough. Besides. you do such a good job of it."

"Sure I do, but there's no reason why you couldn't learn. It's not just drudgery, but a chance to think and focus your thoughts while your hands are doing something worthwhile. But you did say you needed some help. What is it?"

Suzy pulled up a chair and sat down, with her chin resting on the back of the chair and her legs grasping the seat like a rider on a horse.

Her mom watched her, smiled and chidingly added, "Sometimes you're so unlike any girl I know, yet I can't help but admire and appreciate the way you do things. I wouldn't have you any other way."

Suzy blushed, at the compliment her mom had just paid her. *Mom, you're such a caring person, always there to encourage me.* She opened her Bible to the tenth chapter of Daniel and read aloud about Daniel's encounter with the man of brilliance, the terror felt by others and the struggles the man was engaged in before arriving to give Daniel a message.

She looked up at her mom and asked, "Why would Daniel be so frightened? He had many visions, survived the burning furnace and walked among the lions in their den. When a brightly shining man approached, he is terrified."

"Oh child, how can you or I understand what it's like to stand in the presence of an angel sent directly from God. The glory of our Maker still lingers with this angelic being. I'm sure it's all that Daniel can do when facing the magnificence of heaven. Besides, Suzy, don't let Pastor Adams hear you saying that Daniel survived the furnace. He wasn't there. It was Shadrach, Meshach and Abednego who walked through the flames and talked with one who appeared to be the Son of God"

"Oh!" *Mom's right. How did I did that wrong?* "I suppose you're right about being in the presence of an angel. I remember how tongue tied I was when I had a chance to meet the Premier and he sure wasn't an angel..."

"Suzy!"

"Mom, I don't mean it like that. I meant he's a man and not glowing brilliantly like burnished bronze."

Both burst into laughter at this. "I see what you mean."

"But Mom, here you have these three in a furnace and suddenly the Son of God appears to them. I know that refers to Jesus but how can he be there in the Old Testament. He hasn't even been born."

"But He is God and as such is eternal. He chose to rescue those three from the furnace."

"Just a moment then. This angel comes from God to give an account of what is yet to come. It's so wonderful and mysterious - Daniel has a hard time grasping it so it's written down. The angel's really saying that the Son of God is coming to rescue us from the furnace and to set us free from the bonds that bind us. Now it makes sense."

Suzy hopped off her chair and bounced around the room, giggling and humming "Jesus loves me". She stopped and gave her mom a big hug. Her mom hugged her back, being careful not to put dough and flour on her daughter.

"Of course, it makes sense. It's the truth and knowing it sets us free. However, enough now, wash your hands and get back in here. I'm going to show you how kneading's one step in the production of fine bread."

-4-

Alarmed, Timmy sat up, straining to hear what had disturbed a sleep filled with nightmares and dark thoughts. He could hear his breath coming quickly and felt his heart racing as he tried to figure out what was wrong. There it was again- a crying so faint that he could hardly hear it. He got up and made his way across the darkened room to the window, which he opened. The silence was as deep as the darkness in this time before the moonrise. Again, he heard something that made him shudder. It sounded like a young girl pleading to be left alone - then a cackle. His hair stood on end. *Emeralda's out there and she's got Suzy.*

He changed into his outdoor winter hiking clothes and grabbed a small backpack into which he threw a change of clothes. He checked the side pocket and saw that his small emergency pack was still in place. Timmy grabbed the water bottle that he had filled before going to bed and put it in the pack. Timmy placed the pack on his back. He opened the closet door, knelt down, and reached into a small opening bringing out a leather pouch. A quick squeeze verified that his bracelet was still inside. He placed the pouch around his neck inside his coat. He quietly made his way to the kitchen where he grabbed a couple of buns and a small block of cheese. Timmy made his way into the yard. He knew this yard so well that he had no problem moving through the dark.

Timmy paused to catch his breath and to listen – there it was, that plaintive plea, off to his left beyond the garden patch. He found the well-used path and struck out in the direction of the sound. Timmy felt something brush his face and knew what it was - the low hanging bough on the evergreen that stood at the corner of the yard. He heard a scuffling noise across the road towards the pond and set out in pursuit.

It was so dark. He wished that the full moon would rise to give some light. Suddenly, Timmy stumbled over something on the path and he fell headlong into crusty snow, scratching his cheek and exposed ear. He heard a muffled cry come from whatever lay on the path. Timmy crawled over and felt the long hair of a girl. The girl moaned. *Suzy.*

"Suzy, are you all right?" He asked in a whisper.

Another mumble - Timmy touched her face. She flinched at the touch - he then felt a cloth around her mouth. *She's been gagged to keep her from yelling or talking.* He knelt over her to remove the gag; he felt his pouch become very heavy on his neck, like a rock. Timmy tried to straighten up; an icy finger touched him between the neck and shoulder. An electric shock surged through him: momentary darkness came over him. Timmy sensed someone pick him up and carry him a short distance. He felt dizzy as he was placed on the ground. Whoever carried him left him alone. He could smell damp earth and feel warm air waft over him. *I'm in Gorn. Emeralda's gone back for Suzy.*

Timmy struggled to get up but realized that though he wasn't unconscious, he also wasn't fully conscious. He was somewhere in between where he had his wits but no control over his body. *Relax, there's nothing I can do right now but I must be ready when the time comes.*

Shortly, Timmy heard the panting of someone working hard and something placed on the ground nearby followed by a sigh of relief from the carrier and a moan from ground level. A cackle made him shiver, “Well you did your part, my little one. He came running, just as I knew he would. Oh! So predictable these little princes, filled with goodness and charity, so eager to be of help to those in distress.”

A deep growl replaced the cackling; Timmy’s blood ran cold. “No one came to rescue me when I was in need. No prince was anywhere near. Instead, I was left to suffer - I had to face the pain on my own.”

Timmy heard Emeralda shuffle off out of earshot. *She’s come to capture both of us. Why? She hates us for interfering in her plans; somehow, this seems more than revenge.* Timmy tried to raise his head but couldn’t. He tried to move his hands towards the pouch but they wouldn’t respond.

Timmy fought off the panic that swept over him. Slow down, don’t be in a hurry. Emeralda’s put me out of action with some spell. She doesn’t want me harmed. Either this’ll go away on its own, or she’ll remove it. I just need to wait for that time to come. I need to remember, I’m not alone.

Timmy heard another moan. *Someone’s in worse condition than I am.* He lay back to consider this dilemma. He heard some noise and realized that Emeralda was returning with a horse and a cart or wagon. It stopped nearby and he heard her approach to pick up Suzy, who groaned. He heard her shuffle off and soon heard her returning. Timmy knew she was about to pick him up; he cringed at the thought of her touching him, remembering the shock he received earlier. He waited and was relieved when nothing happened as she lifted him.

Timmy heard her breath labouring as she carried and placed him on the floor of the wagon. He wanted to say something but he sensed a restraining finger. *This is not the time. I probably couldn't have spoken anyway.* Emeralda moved away and then the floor tilted slightly as she had boarded the vehicle. As the wagon jerked into motion, a wave of darkness flooded over him - he lost consciousness.

-5-

Timmy woke up when the wagon stopped. He felt the shift in weight as Emeralda slowly climbed off. He could tell the moon was shining; he still couldn't move his head, not even his eyes. However, he could hear the many sounds about him very clearly - the occasional snort from the horse, the quiet hum of insects overhead, and the slow breathing of Suzy.

"Come, come little one. I'm disappointed in you. You certainly can't be made of strong material if you're this injured from falling down that embankment. I warned you not to try to escape. Here, I've some water and a tonic for you. It'll give you strength. Easy does it…, not so fast…."

Timmy heard a bout of coughing and sputtering; he assumed Suzy had swallowed wrong. Emeralda snorted. "I warned you. Now, let's do it again. Easy now, just take a few sips of this. It'll make you feel better. That's it. Now let me put you down, rest a while."

Timmy tensed up. Emeralda will be paying me a visit next. I hope I don't have to go through that shocking experience again. I won't put up with it. Unable to move, he felt helpless. He heard her footsteps drawing near. Emeralda lifted him into a sitting position. He was relieved at the lack of pain. He felt a flask pushed between his lips and teeth and felt the cool soothing flow of a liquid. Water.

"There you go now, little prince, precious prince. Drink slowly. I don't want to harm you. You need to know that

Emeralda only wants the best for you. There's many great and glorious adventures ahead for you, I can tell. With me as your guide, you'll go much further than what those others would allow you to do. Please, forgive me for this time of discomfort – soon, you'll know I have your best interests at heart. Now take it easy as I give you another drink. This'll give you strength, nourishment and rest for the journey ahead."

As he rolled that last comment over in his head, Timmy dreaded what was to come. His mouth was forced open by another bottle and a bittersweet fluid was poured down his throat. He felt revulsion as it burned its way down into his stomach but was powerless to prevent this invasion. Timmy felt himself being forced back down on to the bed of the wagon. He heard Emeralda climbing back into the driver's seat and the soft whisper to the horse to begin moving. He tried to stay alert by focussing on what was happening but he felt groggy, as he sank into a deep sleep.

-6-

Suzy sat up suddenly from a deep and dreamless sleep, sensing something was wrong. It took a few moments for her to realize where she was. She had a deep discomfort as she gazed around the darkened room. Then Suzy heard a faint tinkling sound. *Something needs my attention.* She paused a moment to say a quiet prayer and to remember what her mother had said earlier. *Knowing the truth sets us free.*

Suzy slipped off the bed and made her way to the window to close the curtains so anyone who might be outside couldn't see in. She had nothing to fear since the moon hadn't risen and it was pitch dark outside. *Still, better safe than sorry.* Suzy edged her way to the dresser where she pulled open the top drawer.

Suzy let out a slow breath as she heard the tinkling sound clearer. She looked around the room from the door to the window. *It's safe, no one's around.* She moved her hand inside the drawer along the top until she reached another small drawer, which she pulled open. Delicately, Suzy reached inside with her fingertips and removed a necklace and a chain. The spherical jewel pulsated with a golden glow and emitted a soothing, tinkling sound. As she fastened the necklace around her neck, the soft sound stopped.

Suzy wondered what to do with the chain and the emerald stud until she felt a slight tingle in her hand where the stud touched it. She closed her hand over the stud and breathed deeply. *Emeralda's nearby, I can feel it.* Her intuition told her to take the chain and stud, so she placed the chain around her neck as well.

Quietly and carefully, Suzy moved about the room finding her hiking clothing. She put a number of items into her tote bag and then made her way down the stairs to the icebox where she picked out a number of food items as well as her trusty water bottle. After packing, she looked around the darkened room before leaving through the kitchen door.

The night air was fresh and the scent of mildewed grass hung in the still air. With a practiced step, she set off down the path that led to the lane. Suzy had a good idea which direction to go, so was undeterred by the scurrying of small animals or the hoot of an owl. She paused at the lane to make a few quick decisions. She heard something down the road towards the pond, in the direction she had already decided to go. Suzy had no idea what was going to happen; she had somehow received a summons and had to go.

Very quietly, Suzy made her way down the lane to the main road. Only then did she pause to say a silent prayer before setting off down the gravel road. She stepped lightly, noticed only by the old owl in the tree top and a small rabbit that crouched by the side of the road, wondering why a young girl would be out at this time of night.

All of Suzy's senses seemed to heighten as she made her way towards the pond. She could smell a slight perfume that lingered in the air; she could hear in the distance someone working hard as if carrying a heavy load. She waited a moment longer to get her bearings and moved in the direction of the sound. *I wonder what I'll do if I come face to face with whoever's making so much noise. Oh well, I'll take care of that when I get there: right now I must move quickly.*

Suzy could feel the necklace pressing on her lower neck - its presence gave her courage as she shuffled along the road as quietly as possible. Every twenty or thirty seconds she paused, listened and then proceeded. *I'm getting closer.*

She stopped; in the dim light, she saw someone on the road just ahead of her. A dark figure reached down and picked up a bundle on the ground. Then the figure moved off the road and there was a short burst of light, which blinded her briefly. Whoever had been on the road had vanished – Suzy moved quickly to the spot where she had seen the dark figure. She felt warmth in the air that hadn't been there before and could smell the scent of flowers, green grass and warm earth. Suzy knew without a doubt that she was following Emeralda. The Sage had been carrying someone and had escaped into Gorn. *She had to have Timmy who now really needs my help. What was it that Emeralda said? Timmy has a destiny and she wanted to help him along that path. I have to hurry if I'm to be of any aid to my friend. But how?*

Suzy had to get to Gorn so she looked about for the entryway. There was no sign of a portal. Emeralda must have power to bridge the two worlds at will. I don't have that power. I entered Gorn through a hole and once through a dream. It's growing brighter - the full moon's rising in the east. Moonlight will definitely help me find a way if there is one.

Suzy glanced around and noticed the ground beginning to shine as the moon's light reflected from its damp surface. *Be calm. Be patient.* Suzy shivered knowing Emeralda was scurrying off with her treasure. *Easy does it, Suzy. Emeralda can't move that quickly with Timmy as a load.*

The evening became brighter as the moon rose above the horizon. My answer's somewhere near by. How I know this I don't know – I just know the answer will show itself. I must keep seeking. Of course, that's it. Seek and ye shall find.

That little verse gave her the assurance she needed and she kept up her search. *What's that over there.*

Suzy spotted a dark patch on a much lighter piece of ground. The patch remained as dark as coal even though the moon produced more light, brightening the night. *I know what it is. It's the square hole, the last of the holes I saw when I first put on the necklace.*

Without hesitation, Suzy stepped towards the area of darkness; since it remained stationary, she walked directly into it.

-7-

Suzy felt a slight flutter as she made the transition into Gorn. It took a brief moment to adjust to her new environment. She could smell the scent of fresh spring earth and the fragrance of new flowers. Suzy realized that the seasons of Gorn often were not the same as at home and that time too did not agree. It didn't surprise her to see the sun just peeking over the horizon. *I have no idea where I am in Gorn and how close I am to Timmy. It doesn't matter. I have to try to find him. Together we can fight Emeralda's evil plans.* She walked in a large circle looking for tracks or some other disturbance that might give her a clue as to where her quarry had gone. It was becoming much lighter out and Suzy could easily see the ground in front of her. Meticulously she moved, turning ever so slightly so that she was making a very wide circle. She found herself climbing a significant rise in the land. *Good, I should be able to see them in the distance.*

Suzy heard the sound of angry birds overhead. She looked up to see a large flock of ravens circling above her, cawing and snapping their wings at her. They circled lower, some diving and pulling away just before colliding with her. Her ears heard a strange hoarse cackling; slowly, Suzy made out a scolding, menacing tirade. "Why are you here? You've no business interfering in Gorn. Go home."

Suzy ducked as one of the birds clipped her bonnet as it flew by. She felt her heart pumping rapidly as she looked around for some shelter. There wasn't anything; she was on the slope of the hill in the open. Suzy grasped for the necklace but her fingers contacted the golden chain with the emerald stud instead. She remembered that Emeralda often flew around in the form of a big black crow. She raised it in the air and a flash of green light brightened the space around her. The ravens croaked and sped away, cawing angrily. The girl let go of the chain, allowing it to slip inside her blouse.

Suzy was disappointed when she reached the crest of the hill. No one was in sight but she did see a road off in the distance. *I'll keep that trail in mind; I might need it after I've finished looking for Timmy's tracks.* Suzy kept her eyes focused on the ground looking for some sign that Emeralda and Timmy had passed this way. Suddenly, she realized that she had completed the circuit and was passing over the same ground that she had previously covered. With a sigh, she turned and walked off in the direction of the trail she had spotted earlier.

When Suzy reached it, she saw that it was a relatively unused cart track. She didn't see any evidence that it had been used recently. *Do I go left or right?* Suzy reached towards her neck and grasped the necklaces with her left hand. She felt nothing. She looked both ways again, turned to her left and started down the trail. *I don't know why I'm going this way – it just feels like the thing to do.*

Suzy was still looking for some sign that this was the path used by Emeralda when she noticed a patch of blue off the path by a grove of trees. Her face broke into a large grin as she recognized her special friend and companion.

"Sapphira, what are you doing here?" Suzy shouted in astonishment. Without waiting for an answer, she rushed forward and tripped on the tangled grass that grew alongside the trail. She collapsed in a heap with her backpack flipping up and hitting the back of her head. She lay still for a moment in order to catch her breath. The lady in blue came forward with long measured strides, her face wearing a big smile at the predicament that Suzy had put herself through. She reached Suzy just as the girl was regaining her feet.

"I hope you're okay, dear friend. That's quite a nasty fall you had. As always, you rush into situations without much regard for where you might be stepping." Sapphira laughed in relief that Suzy appeared to be okay.

Suzy blushed. Suzy threw her arms around her friend. Sapphira gave her a short hug. She surveyed her young friend searching for any injury that might go overlooked. Convinced that all was well, she smiled.

Suzy was overjoyed to see her friend. It's hard to be quiet and wait for Sapphira to speak first. As she looked at her friend, she realized how much she looked like Emeralda. It makes sense since they are sisters. What's really strange is that Sapphira's so generous and helpful while Emeralda's greedy and hurtful. She shuddered. Marlen told me that Emeralda wasn't always that way.

"You seem to be all right, Suzy. You asked me a question and it deserves an answer. Why am I here? Actually, I'm looking for you. Marlen asked me to come to you since he knew you were on your way. I'm not sure how he knew but that doesn't matter. He couldn't meet you and wondered if I would. Since I wasn't busy and really missed you, I agreed. Since it's been quite some time since your last visit, you must have a good reason for returning. Of course, I'm thrilled that you have but I wonder why you come now."

"Oh Sapphira, you can't begin to imagine how delighted I'm to see you. I've missed you so much since the last time

I was here. I notice that you've sneaked in a question while saying that you would refrain from asking one."

Both laughed as they stood facing each other. Suzy gave in to her impulse and hugged Sapphira around her neck. It took only a moment for her formal friend to soften and envelope Suzy in a heartfelt hug. They maintained that embrace for a short while after which they released and stepped back from each other.

"Since you asked, I will tell you why I am here."

"But I never asked…"

"Oh, but you did." They laughed again.

Sapphira finally took control of the situation. "Well, I do want to know why you're here. You don't make a habit of popping into Gorn. Even by your time, it's been a while since you were last here."

"Oh, Sapphira, it's Emeralda again. She came to see Timmy and me, just the other day. She looked at Timmy and made it clear she wanted him for some journey. During the night, I heard my necklace chiming and I knew something was wrong. When I went to investigate, I heard Emeralda carrying something. I know she has Timmy. I can't explain that but she has him - he's in some sort of trouble because he wouldn't go with her willingly."

"Well, that's your opinion, little one. He may have been convinced to go with her. He can make up his own mind, you know. Emeralda's very cunning and can sweeten any offer. Still, I suppose you're right. She likely coerced Timmy into it. You didn't see anything else"

"Actually I didn't see much since it was the middle of the night, but I did hear a lot. Come to think about it, there may have been someone or something else there as well. Emeralda was carrying something and she came back for more. Did she take someone else into Gorn? That doesn't make much sense, does it?"

"It's always hard to make sense out of anything that Emeralda does. However, don't for a minute think that her actions are without purpose or that she's simply acting out of spite. She has a reason for everything she does. We may find it hard to figure out or be disgusted with the reason. That's what makes her so dangerous. Maybe, she had someone as bait for Timmy. If she made it look like she'd captured you, Timmy definitely would have come to rescue you. Obviously, she couldn't capture you - she lacks power over you, even in your home world. Did Timmy know that, likely not, or he acted impulsively?"

"Really! You think she nabbed someone else and made it look like she had me instead? That ruse could fool Timmy long enough for him to be captured. Sure, that has to be it. But why would Timmy fall for it? He's smarter than that."

"Yes, Suzy, he's smarter than that but he's young and impulsive. He didn't stop to think it out. He would've thought it was you and acted quickly. Don't be too harsh. You ran off into the night, didn't you?"

Suzy sighed, "Yes, I did. Yes, Timmy would react like that because he'd want to keep me safe. And yes, it was the middle of the night and he wouldn't've been able to see that it wasn't me."

"There! I think we now know what may have happened. Emeralda used Timmy's loyalty to you to force him into action. He never stood a chance against her. She's much more experienced than either of you; her abilities have been honed for longer than you can imagine. She's a formidable foe - one that can never be underestimated."

"I know that much about her. I also know that she bit off more than she can chew when she captured Timmy. He's a fierce opponent and I wouldn't want to be in her shoes, especially if he's been tricked into this. He'll be a handful."

Sapphira laughed. "So I've discovered about both of you. You may very well be right but she still has him captured."

"Exactly! Let's get going to stop her."

"That won't be easy. We don't know where she is."

"She can't be far away. She came into Gorn just before I did. I was looking on this path for some trace of her."

It was Sapphira's turn to sigh. "Did you come through the same portal that she did?"

Suzy paused for a moment, wondering at the question. "No, she made her own and I couldn't find it so I looked around, I saw the square one that I'd seen a long time ago and I went through it."

"Don't you remember what Marlen told you about time here and there? It's not the same; neither are locations through different portals, even if they're located near each other. When Emeralda went through, she came out in a different part of Gorn. We don't know where that is… yet."

"So what happens next?"

"I think we should go back to the palace and talk to Marlen. He can help in this affair."

"That means that we have to leave Timmy in the clutches of that wicked woman. I hate to think of what she'll do to him"

Sapphira placed her hand on Suzy's shoulder. "It's not as bad as you may think. You just said that Timmy's quite capable of looking after himself. I have a great deal of confidence in his ability to handle the situation. In addition, that wicked woman, as you called her, isn't going to harm him. She wants something from him. She needs him and so he has that advantage he can use."

"I know you're right. I just hate to give up looking for him. All right, we need to find Timmy some other way; let's start for the palace. We can talk more as we go."

Suzy and Sapphira walked down the path in the direction that Suzy had been travelling. At the crest of the hill that they were climbing the land stretched out before them in a level plain that consisted of grasslands interspersed with groves of trees. Suzy paused and sucked in the fresh air, admiring the beautiful landscape that lay before them. They continued along the path until they reached a fork in the road. Sapphira chose the right path, which made its way down to the plain.

Suzy looked up at her companion. "How did you know where to find me?"

"Marlen called me and said that he'd received a signal that you might need some help. The signal came from beyond the realm of Gorn and meant you were coming here. He told me to hurry here where the square portal would allow you to enter."

"He knew that I entered through the square portal?"

"Certainly, my dear. You'd already used the oval and the triangle. That was the only one left."

"That's right. Does this mean that there aren't any more portals for me to enter Gorn? That'd mean this is my last trip here."

"I highly doubt that. Your life seems to be closely intertwined with that of Gorn – I'd guess that you've only used up the original three that were tied to the necklace. Remember, you also entered through the fortune teller's ball."

"You know about that!"

"I'm a Sage, my dear. That means I need to know about what goes on in this world. You've grown greatly in your power, even if you're unaware of how much. You'll find other ways of making the jump from your world to ours and back again. Right now, that's not important since you're here. Let's stop for a short break, to have a drink of water and a snack. Then we'll head for the palace which is a good half day's walk from here."

"Half a day?" Suzy removed her backpack to fetch her needed items. "You set off that long ago and I've only been here a short time." Suzy paused, remembering about the time differences. "Oh, what's the palace like? Have things changed very much? How's Blog doing?"

"Well, it sounds like things are getting back to normal, with all your questions." Sapphira laughed. "Yes the signal gave me time to reach you; time is different here. The palace is beautiful; repairs have fixed the damage from the battles. Things have changed, yes indeed, and Blog's part of it. You'll see for yourself once we get there. Come on, rest a few minutes and then we'll be on our way."

The two sat on a large rock located beside the path. They began to snack on their provisions; Suzy fidgeted in anticipation of the journey ahead. *Blog's part of the change; this I have to see.*

-8-

Timmy heard a moan, which made him alert, as he woke from a deep sleep. He tried to shake his head to clear cobwebs in his head but couldn't. *I've been drugged so that I'd sleep and not know where we were going.* He didn't feel any movement from the wagon on which he was riding. It was early morning because the sky was a deep blue and the birds were singing. Timmy listened and could hear Suzy breathing nearby; it wasn't restful breathing but one filled with catches and gasps. He would be able to help if only he could move his arms. *Oh, I'm so helpless. Emeralda touched me and now I can't move. She must have placed a spell on me. I don't know anything about spells. What I do know is that Suzy's hurting and I can't help her.*

Timmy relaxed and concentrated on finding a way to overcome his problem. It was then that he remembered what he learned during Bible lessons; 'I am the way and the truth and the life,' and 'I tell you the truth; anyone who has faith in me will do what I have been doing. He will do even greater things than these.' Timmy felt so much more at ease.

So I've been trying to do it on my own. I'll pray that the Lord will use me in this circumstance.

Timmy realized shortly that he could move his eyes and look to the side. He then tried turning his neck and was able to see to the right where Suzy lay facing away from him. He raised his bound hands, touched Suzy on the head and felt her flinch. *She doesn't know it's me.*

Timmy whispered, "Relax! Let me help you. I'll rest my hands on you and the pain will go away."

He again touched her on her head and could feel that she was trembling uncontrollably, whimpering in dread. He didn't understand why Suzy would be in such a state. He relaxed and waited; she began to relax and become quiet. Timmy sensed her pain leaving as her breathing became deeper and less laboured. He waited another few seconds and then removed his hands, feeling relief that Suzy was on the mend.

"Who are you?"

The question baffled him. "Suzy, it's me, Timmy. Are you all right?"

Timmy sat up, waiting as Suzy struggled to sit up. As she turned, he was surprised to find himself looking at a face that was not Suzy's. He didn't know what to say.

The girl who sat there asked, "What's going on? Where am I? Who are you? Why did you call me Suzy? How did you get rid of my pain? Who's that horrid old woman? How can we get away?" Her eyes grew larger with each question as Timmy watched her becoming more bewildered and frightened.

"Easy does it. I'll try to answer some of your questions but please relax. My name's Timmy. I thought you were a good friend of mine named Suzy. I now see that I was wrong. That old woman's a fearful enemy who's been trying very hard to gain control over me. Now it seems she has, by using you as a decoy, knowing that I'd come to the rescue of my good friend. I think she drugged and carried us off. What else was there? Oh, yes, I have the power of healing. I wasn't able to use it until I surrendered my will. I believe you're feeling better now."

"Yes, I am. How'd I get into this?" The red-haired girl paused and stared at Timmy, putting her hand over her mouth. "Now I remember. I was on my way home from school. That old woman came up behind me with the horse and wagon. She asked if I wanted a ride home. I should've known better than to climb up there with her. She grabbed me and began to tie up my hands. I struggled, broke free and started to run away. She yelled at me to be careful but I wasn't watching where I was going and suddenly pitched forward over a steep embankment. I fell, rolled, and tumbled to the bottom and I could feel a sudden pain in my leg as I struck a rock on my way down.

When I tried to get up, I found that my leg hurt too much. I was helpless as she brought the wagon near and lifted me on board. She was jabbering all the time about my foolishness and awkwardness. She said. 'You're really not a very good substitute but you'll have to do if I'm to be successful.'

She gave me something to drink. I gagged, but it also made me groggy. I tried to scream for help but she covered my mouth. I remember being carried a few times as I drifted in and out of consciousness. I do remember the pain remained with me until a few minutes ago. I just want to go home. Please let me go."

"I'm not the one keeping you here. However, there's a serious problem. I know we aren't in your homeland. We've been carried into a strange and different place called Gorn. In many ways, it's like home, but here magic plays a bigger role. Right now, I need your help. I'll untie your hands and then I want you to do the same for me. Please, don't try to run away.

I can see it in your eyes. Please, help me and then we can help each other." Timmy held up his tied hands.

"I can't stay here. I can't stand her."

"I know you're confused, scared and unsure of what to do. Don't run away. I don't know where we are. Neither do you. You'll be lost and maybe even captured by far worse than Emeralda…, oh, by the way, that's her name. She's dangerous, she's wicked, she's smart and has many powers. She even cast a spell over me. However, she knows where we are; because of that, we need her. Now, promise me, if I untie your hands, you won't run. By the way, who are you?"

"My name's Tasha. I suppose you're right about getting lost. I wouldn't be in this fix if I'd listened to what I've been told many times about strangers. But you're a stranger too so why should I listen to you?"

"You have to be the judge. Remember, I've helped you already, Tasha."

Tasha looked at him, obviously weighing what he said. Then she heaved a sigh. "Okay, okay! I won't freak out on you and charge off leaving you on your own. I'm sure you likely need some help from me."

She held out her hands. Timmy took the bindings into his fingers and worked them loose. A moment later Tasha was wriggling her hands out of what had seemed an impossible situation. As the ropes fell to the wagon bed, she dropped Timmy's hands and looked around them. She scanned the area and then winked at Timmy.

"Got you nervous yet?"

"Not really." He lifted his hands and held them out for her. Surprisingly, she was as dexterous in undoing the knots as Timmy had been. She smiled as he showed a bit of surprise.

"I go with Dad sailing and he has shown me many knots and how to work with them. I'm not an invalid, even if I did get myself into this pickle."

Timmy rubbed his wrists and then flexed his fingers. He stood up on the wagon and looked around. He reached out his hand to Tasha and helped her to stand up. She placed weight on her right leg, the one that had been injured. "You did a good job healing it, that's what you said. It feels as good as always. I must say I'm impressed. How did you do that?"

"Really, I don't actually know. I discovered that I can place my hands on someone who's sick or injured and they experience a healing." *I'm not going to mention that the first time I noticed this was when we found the bracelet that badly burned Suzy's finger.*

Tasha took his hands in hers, looked at the palms and then the back of each hand. "They look normal. It's hard to believe that they can heal. I find it hard to believe even though my pain went away when you touched me." She smiled at Timmy. "Thank you so very much. I'm so glad you didn't know I wasn't your friend or I'd still be in pain."

"You're welcome and wrong. I'd never leave you suffering like you were. I'd have healed you, no matter what."

"Yes, I'm sure you would've, even if I don't know why."

"Tasha, if you're in need I'm called to help you. You remember the Golden Rule. For me it's an imperative. I've even helped enemy soldiers who'd intended to injure me. I don't know why I have this gift, but I do know that I'm to use it to ease suffering, any suffering, whenever I can."

"Well I'm grateful and I'll say it again. Thank you. Now, we've a much bigger problem to solve. We should go through the food supply and take what we need on our journey out of here. We should set out quickly." Tasha looked over her shoulder as if trying to scout out the area.

"That we can't do. We're somewhere in the middle of Gorn and the only one who knows where is our captor."

"But you said you've been here before. Surely, you remember how you got back home." Tasha bit her nails.

"Oh I remember how I went home the last time I was in Gorn but I've never been in this spot before. I'm as lost as you are."

"How can you be so calm about it? Aren't you worried? What are we going to do now?" Tasha waved her hands in the air.

"I'm calm because right now there's nothing I can do. I'm not going to fret about it. I am worried about why we're here but I can wait for that answer. I believe what we do next is wait. We wait for Emeralda to return because she's our ticket out of here." Timmy glanced around.

"Boy! She's going to be surprised to see us up and waiting for her. It'll do her good to see that her plans are messed up." Timmy climbed down from the wagon and stretched his legs.

Tasha followed him. "Oh, I suppose you're right although I don't like it. I don't look forward to her snatching and tying us up on the wagon and giving us that awful drink. Ugh! That was terrible!"

"Oh, she won't be doing that again, I can assure you of that. She may have got the jump on us before but now she has a handful. Let's gather some twigs, start a campfire, and cook up some food. I'm famished." Timmy began to look around for firewood.

Tasha went through the supplies and soon they had a thick porridge bubbling in a pot over a small fire. They pulled up some larger logs to sit on. Timmy had just risen to stir the pot when Emeralda appeared from behind a small knoll. Tasha gasped and clenched her hands together. Timmy continued towards the pot. Emeralda frowned to see the two of them moving around.

As she approached, Timmy stirred the pot. "You look like you've seen a ghost, Emeralda. Maybe you're surprised to find us here and free, or should I say, free and here." He chuckled as he tended to the food.

When Tasha saw how nonchalantly Timmy was acting, she gained a bit of boldness. "We've been waiting for you to come back so that we could eat together. We certainly have lots to talk about."

Timmy gave her a thumbs-up signal that Emeralda couldn't see. *Good girl, you might actually be a good ally to have if you can pull yourself together to stand up to this foe.*

Emeralda looked around to see if there was anyone else nearby. Timmy thought he could see some confusion in the Sage and no wonder - how the two of them could be free since she had bound them herself. She warily approached, watching the two prisoners very closely. Timmy showed no effects of the spell he had been under and the girl did not look injured at all.

Emeralda stepped confidently as she grew nearer. Timmy could see the subtle change in her approach. *Wily witch, putting on an act, are you now? Be careful.*

Timmy took the bowl offered by Tasha and spooned it full of porridge. He gave Tasha a slight nod in the direction of Emeralda. She replied with a smile, as if to say, this is going to be interesting. She held the bowl out to the lady in black, who suddenly came to a stop. Emeralda hesitated and then took the bowl from the girl.

Timmy filled two more bowls and went to sit across from Tasha on the log. They began to eat the porridge as Emeralda stood there, holding her bowl, watching.

-9-

Suzy and Sapphira set out after their lunch. Time slipped away quickly as they walked over the plain towards a small wooded area. Sapphira slowed her walk and began to look around.

"Stop for a moment, Suzy. I'm going to cast a spell to see if anything is nearby."

Before Sapphira was able to raise her staff three large black bears charged from the trees towards them. Sapphira raised her staff; the bears separated and continued to run toward the two travellers. A bolt of blue light erupted from the staff and struck the first bear, causing it to stumble and collapse.

Suzy grasped her necklace. The spherical gem emitted a red light, the flash catching the second bear. It rolled over, whimpering.

Another bolt of blue light struck the remaining bear and it slid to a stop about three feet from Sapphira and Suzy. The Sage slowly walked around each bear, looking at the downed animal. She waved to Suzy.

"Let's keep going. They'll be out of action for about a half hour and then they'll need to find a drink. There's a creek just through these trees. We'll be long gone."

Suzy looked at the beasts and then followed Sapphira down the path. Sapphira turned to Suzy. "Are you all right?"

"I'm fine, although they did scare me."

"I'd better pay more attention to our journey and less to our talking. They shouldn't've got so close. I see how your necklace comes to your aid."

Over the next two hours, they walked many miles; Suzy knew Sapphira was measuring her steps so she could keep up.

Sapphira glanced over at Suzy. "Maybe we should watch for a place where we can stop for a little rest to regain our strength."

"You don't have to stop on my account." Suzy struggled to get the words out. She was tired but wanted to get to the Palace.

"Let's watch for a spot. It would give us a chance to talk again."

Suzy looked up and saw a rest area ahead as they rounded a bend in the road. "Look! There seems to be a natural spot to stop. We'll be able to put up our feet and rest for a few minutes. You can tell me what's going on in Gorn. I haven't heard anything from Gorn - except that Emeralda said she's being hounded by some wild character."

They made their way to the benches, which were set around a flat rock that served as a table or a footrest. Suzy sat down. Sapphira smiled as she too sat down.

Suzy caught the Sage's reaction. "Yes, I know, I said I was willing to keep on."

Suzy reached into her pack for a water bottle and a piece of cheese. *Both look so good right now.*

Sapphira leaned back and looked at Suzy preparing her lunch - she seemed to be far away in thought.

Suzy looked up, noticing Sapphira deep in thought. "What's been happening since I was here last?"

"Well, things have settled down since you rid the land of the growing darkness and banished their commander. The dark forces have retreated deep into their country and haven't made any major excursions out of their hideout. Oh! Certainly, they continue to send out spies, many of who are captured and questioned; some reveal important information. Apparently, the dark lord, Natas himself, has taken control of the forces because you defeated Chrane's commander. Chrane has lost his command as well to Natas. Natas is pure evil with a cunning mind and a single purpose - the complete subjugation of all of Gorn."

"That's awful." Suzy frowned.

"So far, the Sages have determined that the dark forces are rebuilding their strength and are being retrained to increase their resolve. Many have paid a heavy price for deserting and fleeing when confronted by you. The remainder now know the price for disloyalty. The foe facing us is far more formidable. We have sent out our own spies to find weak points in our lines. There have been no major skirmishes so our forces have had a chance to recover, to grow in strength and in health, and train for the future."

"How's Blog doing? The last time I saw him he had a small band of soldiers who were devoted to him. He was such an amazing fellow. At first, he seemed like a clumsy oaf but he grew in stature and displayed fantastic leadership ability. Who would have guessed?" Suzy tapped her lips.

"Indeed, who would have guessed? I'll get back to Blog shortly. Emeralda has divided the Sages' attention, as always. She continues to be a thorn in our side and she's always one step ahead of us. Our efforts to capture her so that we can try some rehabilitation always come up short. Emeralda's continually drawn back to the Castle of the lodestone. We have felt her presence near it several times. When we get a group together to go there she has seemingly vanished, only to turn up far away."

"Then why not post a guard and wait for her - when she comes near the lodestone you can capture her?

"That seems like the easiest way to do it, doesn't it. Suzy, we can't spare the Sage power away from the front lines for that length of time and she knows it. So the game of cat and mouse continues. We can't afford to have her near the stone. She might come up with a way to retrieve it so we have to send a group to drive her away. Then, we can't stay so we come back to the front and she returns. Now you tell me Emeralda's captured Timmy; I'm sure it has something to do with the lodestone. We'll have to increase our vigilance since she's likely to try again to gain control over it. She's driven by her obsession."

Suzy didn't say anything for a long time - Sapphira sat looking over the scene before her. The Sage seemed lost in thought but Suzy knew that she was as alert as ever; nothing would catch them unawares. *It must be such a burden to have Emeralda as a sister and a foe.*

Sapphira ruerned her gaze to her friend. "Well, enough of that, Suzy. Your dear friend, Blog, has turned out to be quite a find for the forces of good. He has an uncanny ability to lead and inspire soldiers to do their best. He's been awarded the rank of general…."

"What! Blog a general? Is he capable?"

"It was the Council of Sages that made the promotion. I think we're able to ascertain the ability level of a competent soldier."

"I suppose so." Suzy blushed.

"I suppose so! Yes! Blog leads the army and has he ever trained the soldiers. They're loyal, devoted to him and would follow him into all kinds of trials."

Suzy jumped to her feet and threw her bag over her shoulder. "Let's get going. I want to see this for myself. I'm so proud of him."

Sapphira set off down the path and walked faster as Suzy kept up to her.

-10-

Timmy and Tasha ate their porridge. Emeralda stood watching them, the bowl of porridge in her hands. Timmy looked up and laughed.

"What's the matter, Emeralda? Aren't you hungry? Are you just going to stand there, holding your food until it gets cold? Ah! I know what the problem is. You think that we may have poisoned your food. Oh yes, Emeralda, Tasha and I have more than enough reason to do just that after the way you treated us. But, don't be silly. We don't intend to hurt you. Give me that bowl. You take mine; I'll eat yours to show you that it's perfectly safe. Not only that, it's quite tasty as well."

He stood up and held out his bowl. Emeralda stepped forward but then caught herself. She turned to the side and sat down. She proceeded to take a spoonful of porridge and put it in her mouth with bravado. She then looked right at Timmy.

"What a silly thought, young master. You think that I'd worry how you might harm me. That's ridiculous. What do you think you could do to me?" She shovelled another spoonful into her mouth and she made a show of chewing it and then swallowing it all in one gulp.

Tasha grinned as she watched her captor trying to act so boldly. She too could see that Emeralda was at a loss about what was going on. She caught Timmy's quick nod.

Emeralda watched her two former captives warily - they seemed so calm under the circumstances. Emeralda saw them keeping distance between each other - getting control was going to be tricky.

Emeralda watched Tasha finish her porridge and get up to pour a cup of water. “So little one, I see you are a trickster. You had me convinced that the tumble had seriously injured you. I’ll bet you even staged that. Do you know how heavy you are? Here you were acting all the time.”

Tasha turned and stared at Emeralda, obviously shocked at the cold assessment of Tasha’s earlier condition. Tasha glared at the Sage as she Tasha set down her cup next to her bowl.

“You’re quite remarkable and ever so observant since you have seen through my attempt at acting injured so easily. I guess I’ll just have to be more careful and perform my act even more realistically. You’ll never know.” Tasha smiled widely and then pursed her lips towards Emeralda.

Timmy was astonished at Tasha’s reaction. He’d worried that she was going to be a liability but he was learning fast that here was a very capable assistant. Tasha had just covered up her sudden healing; this removed any need to explain it to Emeralda, something that would have been difficult without revealing the truth. Not only that, but Tasha had now tossed the ball back into Emeralda’s court and left her more confused than before. She won’t know whether to believe Tasha or not. *This is going to be good. Still, we have to be very careful. This is Emeralda and she’s as cunning as a fox and as dangerous as a viper.*

Timmy saw Emeralda watching Tasha’s movements while noting his whereabouts. He decided to check this out by changing his position. He stood up and stretched. Emeralda became more alert. He moved about and watched Emeralda track his movements and Tasha’s. Timmy moved over towards Tasha in order to set his bowl down where she left hers.

Emeralda watched closely, her eyes following Timmy as she continued to eat the porridge. and knew that if she was to have any chance over the two of them, she had to act when they were near to each other. She took another spoonful of porridge. *My goodness, this is good!* She caught herself and rebuked her diversion of attention. *It's only porridge. Stay focussed. I want to be successful.*

Timmy was amused by how Emeralda seemed to be enjoying her porridge, but he also saw Emeralda preparing to move as he approached Tasha. He changed direction, put his bowl down on a seat instead of beside the pot and then stepped farther from Tasha. He watched Emeralda relax and resume her watching. *Emeralda's waiting for us to be close together*. He had get Tasha in the know. He saw her looking his way and did a quick nod and flicker of his eyes. Tasha winked as she saw his signal. He gave a slight twitch of his index finger towards Emeralda and again Tasha winked an acknowledgement. Timmy was pleased that she was on the ball. He moved around the table.

Emeralda finished her food without losing sight of the young people and then she set down her bowl. Foolish little prince, do you take me for some dope who's not capable of seeing what you're doing. So little ones, you hope to catch Emeralda napping, do you? Wait until I have you bound again. You won't like what I have in store for you.

Timmy kept his eyes on the Sage. *I have to force her hand without getting caught. I don't want a repeat of what happened earlier.*

"So, Emeralda, what's your purpose in bringing us here? If I'm not mistaken it has something to do with the lodestone, doesn't it?" Timmy hoped that Emeralda would be more at ease and release some valuable information.

Emeralda looked up at him. "My little prince, you really haven't any idea how great you could be. I've told you this before; you have a destiny of greatness. But, you wouldn't listen. That Suzy kept you from seeing what could be. That's why I had to get you away from her. She doesn't want you to succeed, that one. She's jealous of your power and always gets in your way of achieving greatness and glory."

"Wrong, Emeralda. Suzy only wants the very best for me. She's always been supportive. You wouldn't know about that because you only think about yourself. Just don't cut her down again." Timmy glared at Emeralda.

"All right, young prince. I can see you like her very much. I won't bring her into this again. You want to know why you're here. I've told you that I want to help you. That's why I brought you here. How many times do I have to repeat myself? You have the chance to become greater. You're wrong when you say that all I think about is myself. I want to support you in your growth as a powerful prince of Gorn."

"You sure have a strange way of wanting to help. You capture us, you put Tasha and me in danger, and you fill us with some vile potion while we're tied up. Let's get down to the truth. Why are we here?"

Emeralda looked at her prey warily. "I've told you why but you don't believe it. You have immense powers that only need to be developed. You have hidden strength that only I, as a Sage, can sense. Yes, young one, don't forget that I'm a Sage. If you put yourself in my hands, I can help you tap into those powers, one of which will give you the ability to open gateways between our worlds. You have so much ahead of you." She smiled. *When I have you in my hands you'll do as I say. You'll grow in power so that I may be greater.*

Timmy could see that he wasn't going to get more from her. *I suppose I'll have to make the first move but it will be on my terms. Tasha and I aren't going lose the advantage we've gained by freeing ourselves. I know what you're waiting for, you old witch. You want to put me under a spell by a neck touch, like the last time. That won't happen again and you'd better not go after Tasha. Careful now, keep your eye on her. She'll be on us in a flash so don't slip up.* He threw a quick glance at Tasha who responded with a nod and then turned away from Emeralda as Timmy approached her.

Emeralda watched as Timmy moved towards Tasha. Now's my chance. Without any thought of a trap, she sprang forward with catlike quickness. I must touch both young people but especially Timmy. I know I can subdue Tasha if Timmy's out of the way. If memory serves me right Timmy will be in a deeper state of immobility, which may be of concern later. Right now, I can't worry about that.

Timmy watched her move. Though he was amazed at her speed, he never lost focus; he watched Emeralda reach out to make contact. She was fast but not fast enough for the young prince. Timmy reached out and seized Emeralda by her wrists.

"No, you don't, Emeralda. Don't you dare touch Tasha again." Timmy looked at Tasha. "Tasha, Quick! Get out of her reach." He held on tightly, surprised at his foe's inability to move.

Emeralda was shocked at Timmy's quick interception. She couldn't believe the jolt of raw energy that hit her when he grabbed her. She felt her spell spiral out of control and bounce back towards her. She was able to cast a counter spell just in time to prevent being hit by the dual spell that she had released. Still, this exercise robbed her of a great deal of power; her strength was drained. The actual physical depletion of energy was nothing compared to the unexpected power in Timmy's hands. She was unprepared for that.

With Timmy standing over her, Emeralda crumbled to her knees. Timmy continued to hold her wrists, knowing that she might be down but by no means was she defeated. Tasha scrambled beyond the campsite and stood, wonderstuck, at the sight of Timmy overpowering Emeralda.

-11-

As Sapphira and Suzy reached the crest of a small hill on the road, they caught sight of the Palace of the Sages. The Palace was nestled in a shallow valley, the slopes of which were heavily treed but carefully cut back to allow a buffer of empty space before the walls. The Palace was of a simple design yet projected elegance. It was a brilliant white structure, inlaid with glass windows that reflected the sunshine, causing it to sparkle like a many faceted jewel. Towering over the Palace were two towers that reminded Suzy of the Pillars from which she freed the Sages. The flickering lights caused Suzy to sigh and reach for the necklace since the appearance of the Palace reminded her of the crystals in her necklace.

"It's beautiful, Sapphira, so beautiful that it almost takes my breath away. It looks like a beautiful gem; in fact, lovelier than any jewel that exists. Oh, it must be wonderful to live here and be able to bathe in the splendour of this place."

"Oh Suzy, sometimes you just go on and on. Yet, you're right. Maybe we who live here take it for granted and don't appreciate and enjoy the magnificence of this place. Often I stand on a hill like this and view the beauty of the Palace and, though it doesn't astound me as you've indicated, I must say that I'm deeply impressed with the brilliance of the Palace. It has caused many to comment on how fortunate we are to have this gem. It's something that everyone who lives here would be willing to fight and die for. Notice the yellow flag on the second tower. Our presence has been noted and the flag was raised to let everyone know that we're on our way."

Suzy turned to Sapphira, looking puzzled. "How would they know this? We haven't been visible long enough for someone to react that fast."

Sapphira smiled. "Remember, we're no longer in your world. A field of spells surrounds this Palace. We crossed the first many miles back and since then, we've been tracked by other spells. Yellow means that we're friendly and of no potential danger. Deep purple would have indicated the presence of a dangerous enemy - a trained force of fighters and a battery of spells from the accompanying Sages would have confronted us. Other colours indicate varying degrees of caution. Even though we travel under the yellow flag of friendship, you'll notice to our right and to our left there are small cohorts of fighters who are moving parallel to our path, keeping us under constant observation. Vigilance is the key to our security and we'll never again allow our Sages to be caught off guard."

Suzy watched the two groups of soldiers marching in the distance. She could see that they were heavily armed and that they camouflaged their purpose by carrying out training drills. *They were not only guarding their Palace but also using the time to improve and maintain the skills that they need for a real enemy.*

"How long have they been marching alongside us? I didn't notice them before. When did they sneak up on us?"

"They began serving as our guard about fifteen minutes ago. You wouldn't have seen them approach since they came out of the woods a ways back and remained out of sight until about three minutes ago. I knew they were there because I sensed their presence through the warning spell I've cast around us so that we wouldn't be caught unaware, like we were earlier by those bears."

"It's amazing how you do these things, Sapphira. I wish I had some of those hidden talents that you have."

"Be careful what you wish for, Suzy. This hidden talent, as you call it, is the result of a lifetime of training of both the physical and the mental self. There are countless hours of regimen involved here. You call it amazing but it's what I've been prepared for all my life. I'm amazed at the abilities that you've displayed in your short life. You've accomplished so much for one so young yet you don't seem to realize how much you've done."

Suzy considered what Sapphira said to her. She had been told many times that she was a princess but exactly what that meant was never made clear. Sapphira said she had undergone intensive training for a long time – suddenly, Suzy realized exactly what that meant. She remembered being told that Emeralda undertook to guard the lodestone for three cycles and each cycle was… one hundred and eleven years. That was… three hundred and thirty-three years. Emeralda had already trained as a Sage when this happened so she must be very old… Sapphira was Emeralda's sister so…. Suzy's eyes widened as she gazed at her friend.

"What is it, my young friend?"

"How old are you, Sapphira?" Suzy blurted out. Then, she caught herself and put her hand over her mouth. She blushed deep red. "Oh, please forgive me, I should know better than to ask without thinking. I'm always doing that and I end up in all kinds of hot water."

"Actually, it's no trouble at all." Sapphira chuckled. "But you must know that it's considered impolite to ask a lady her age, especially one who's obviously quite old."

"But you don't look or act old. Until I started to put some facts together I never even thought about your age."

"Suzy, that's the reason why we've trained so thoroughly. It's to prepare us always to be alert, to observe, to remember, to analyze and to synthesize based on what we've learned. We're always considering what we've heard and learned so that we make sound decisions without being hurried. We're trained to display wisdom. It's an ongoing process that requires immense study and continued training."

"Sapphira, you say that you've undergone long periods of training. How much of your life have you devoted to this exercise? How much study do you do and where do you do it?"

The two of them continued walking towards the Palace. Their guards moved closer but kept a discrete distance so as not to disturb the privacy of their conversations. The soldiers in each group maintained a stony gaze forward as their commanders shouted directions but they still found time to keep the pair of women under surveillance.

Sapphira broke the silence as she turned to Suzy. "Training is of many kinds. First, we're part of the army where we improve our physical well-being, coordination and agility but also learn to rely on the efforts of the group. A Sage must display wisdom for the group around him or her. None of this training is for our own advancement or wellbeing. It's to make each of us the best helper or servant for those in need. We also are taught spells and then given opportunities to train in their use. We study the great Sages of the past in the libraries that are located in the Sage palaces throughout Gorn. However, life is not just training and study. There've been many assignments to duty requiring the efforts and skills of the Sages. We've fought battles against the dark forces and healed those injured in those battles. We have constructed spells and barriers to keep evil out, or at least contained in controlled areas, of Gorn."

"That would also include the work that you do in guarding the lodestone. You would've been involved with that. You must have been involved during the time when Emeralda took possession of the lodestone and held it with the help or her assistant, Ebony."

"Yes, the Sages developed the lodestone as a weapon against the dark forces. A great deal of our power and spells went into its creation. We have to guard the stone to prevent the dark forces from gaining control over it and turning its power against us. I too had a cycle with it and I too felt the immense strain of being close to it. One session was enough for me, but the Sages asked Emeralda to guard it three times." Sapphira shook her head.

"Oh, what a terrible responsibility we Sages bear for having allowed Emeralda more than one watch. However, we were so preoccupied with the fight against Chrane that we didn't fully consider all the ramifications. We chose unwisely and tragedy came to our council. Emeralda was lured into a life that has been a loss to us. I lost a sister…." Sapphira paused for a long moment before she continued. "But more importantly we lost a Sage, one who was powerful, one who was kind, and one who was a true leader. The Council continues to mourn her loss and finds it difficult to operate without her. She makes matters worse when her activities run counter to our work."

"Why do you allow her to do that? Can't you just capture her? She has caused more than enough trouble. I don't understand why you let her go on doing all these things." She then added with downcast eyes, "I'm sorry again because this must be quite difficult for you considering that she's your sister. Have you tried healing her?"

"When you use the word 'you' I believe you mean the Council?" Sapphira asked and waited for Suzy's slight nod of agreement before continuing. "As I said before, Emeralda's very powerful, very knowledgeable, and very crafty. She's a Sage and as such can use the mindlink to determine our movements. Of course, it also means that we can track her's as well so she avoids using mindlinks. She's no ordinary foe. Emeralda's always several steps ahead of us. Moreover, her motives govern her movements, which mean she acts quite randomly and unexpectedly. We had her in a prison but we were drained emotionally and physically by that action. Since her escape, we haven't been able to lure her into a trap. She has evaded capture, not that we've tried very hard. The Council feels deeply responsible; we have decided that she can roam around freely, provided she isn't a direct hazard to the safety and wellbeing of Gorn. As for healing, we tried that while she was in our custody. We thought we'd succeeded but the damage was too deep. I haven't been able to communicate with her since. Emeralda avoids me in particular, as if I'm the real danger to her. I've only seen her at a distance and always fleeing from my presence."

"I wish I could help somehow."

"But you have, my dear, you've been of great assistance. Never play down the role you've accomplished."

"Oh I know that," Suzy interrupted, "but everyone in Gorn has a purpose and knows what it is. Here I am, a young, foolish girl who's always babbling on without making any sense and showing up unexpectedly."

"You are young; you have years to experiment and try new things. Don't wish to be burdened with the responsibilities of adults. You have great potential and you've already tapped into some of it. I sense you have a life of excitement and wonder ahead of you. What form it takes I can't tell but circumstances, choices and the movements of others will determine where you end up. Such is the way of the world."

"I said it before and I'll say it again; I think training to be a Sage would be wonderful."

"If you're called to be a Sage you'll have countless years of study and training before you became the greatest Sage that Gorn has had, but I don't believe that's your calling. In fact, I sense that the time of Sages is fading."

"No, no, Sapphira, don't say things like that. You're needed here. Don't talk about fading." Suzy glanced around and saw that the soldiers had overheard her outburst. For a brief moment, they turned to look her way but quickly snapped back to attention.

"Suzy, I believe that I'll be around for a long time so don't worry that I might fade away before your eyes." She laughed. "We're almost there - look who's coming this way to greet you."

Suzy looked up and was pleased to see Marlen coming down the path from the palace. At once, she forgot her good intentions to act dignified, not impulsively. She ran towards her approaching friend. This, of course, caused some consternation among her guards as they broke into a measured fast march to keep up to her. Many of the soldiers wore broad smiles on their faces as they remembered the impetuousness of youth.

-12-

Marlen waited with a huge smile on his face as Suzy ran towards him. She was oblivious to the activity around her - the soldiers continued their hurried pace to keep up to her and Sapphira increased her stride. Suzy grinned from ear to ear. Marlen stood in the middle of the path, wearing a long flowing azure-blue robe, embroidered with symbols of the sun, moon and stars. This time he wore a brimless skullcap, which bore similar but smaller emblems. He stood with his feet apart and with his right hand slightly raised and his left at his side.

Suzy came to an abrupt halt just before Marlen and stood still, smiling, not saying a word.

Marlen chuckled. "Are you just going to stand there, staring or are you going to give me a hug?"

Suzy squealed and ran into his upraised arms. He hugged her.

"It's good to see you, Marlen. Sapphira said you'd be waiting. I never expected she meant quite literally out here on the path. Oh, Marlen, so much has happened since I last saw you. To tell you would take too long but the most critical is that Timmy has been captured. We must rescue him right away. Emeralda has him; we don't know where but she'll do him harm if we don't act quickly."

"Not so fast, little one. Catch your breath and relax for a minute - let me enjoy this moment. My, my, still so spontaneous! Here, let me have a look at you."

Marlen stepped back a pace, "My goodness! You have grown since I saw you last." Marlen glanced around. "Look at all the commotion you've caused without even knowing it. This often happens. We don't realize the ripples on the pond of life that we create by our seemingly little and insignificant movements. These ripples spread out affecting all with whom they come in contact. The effects can range from insignificant to life changing."

Suzy saw the two groups of soldiers rapidly approaching. They seemed intent on moving much closer than they were before. She could see that all the soldiers were flushed from their hurried march. She saw Sapphira walking much quicker than before. Suzy blushed at the thought that her sudden and unexpected run had brought all this about.

Marlen held up his finger. "No, Suzy, please don't apologize for being yourself. We all appreciate you for who you are. It's your free spirit that enables you to be the powerful princess you've shown you are."

The first group of soldiers came to an ordered stop just before them. The commander stepped forward and saluted Suzy and Marlen by placing his right hand over his heart. "We're at your command. Princess, you bring our company great joy because escorting you is an honour. Would you allow these loyal men the opportunity to salute you?"

Suzy looked surprised at the request and turned to Marlen for advice. He smiled and nodded his head. Suzy turned to the commander as the second group of soldiers came to a stop behind the first group. "Sir, it is I who am honoured by your presence. Of course, I'll accept your salute."

The two companies came to attention and then simultaneously saluted her with their right hands over their hearts. Then they all broke into broad smiles and cheered her. Suzy returned the salute and smiled.

Marlen stepped forward and spoke to the commanders of the two groups. “Thank you for your escort. You’ve completed your assigned task; now, Sapphira and I will act as protectors for the princess. You may take your leave and return to the palace.”

The commanders backed up and faced their men. They gave a “quick march” command and the soldiers marched off without a glance towards Suzy. She stood watching them leave and marvelled at the precise movement of the groups. “Marlen, these soldiers have such order and discipline.”

“Oh yes, little one. The soldiers are dedicated to being well-trained and highly disciplined. All this is due to our friend, Blog, who’s proven to be a tremendous and dedicated leader.”

“Really, Marlen! Blog’s responsible for all this. It’s amazing!”

“Oh, it’s more than that. Blog has proven to be an invaluable asset for our forces. Under his watch, the soldiers have become a solid military machine, which obeys his every command with the highest degree of admiration and respect. Just think of what Timmy and you are responsible for. You found him as a belligerent, fearful, undisciplined soldier and, through your trust and care, he’s developed his abilities.”

“I can hardly wait to see him.”

“I hope you won’t start running again.” Sapphira arrived beside Marlen. “It’s difficult to keep up to you when you take off like that.”

The three companions laughed. Suzy felt at ease being together with these two again. She smiled and then suddenly remembered the danger that Timmy was facing.

"Marlen, you must help Timmy right now. Emeralda has him as a prisoner."

"Suzy, take it easy." Marlen placed his hand on her shoulder for a moment. "We're aware that Emeralda has made a move against Timmy. We've long anticipated this would happen. It's her nature to try every prince and princess. Right now, we don't know where she is."

"Oh Marlen, we must find them. I'm so frightened."

"Easy, Suzy. Remember, this is Timmy. He has shown his ability in the past. He has hidden powers and strengths that we know he can call on. Emeralda will have her hands full"

Suzy laughed briefly. "Oh, I know Timmy and he's going to be really upset with being captured. I trust he'll come out on top. Emeralda has bitten off more than she can chew. Oh, I hope so."

Marlen and Sapphira both placed a hand on Suzy's shoulder as they walked up the path towards the palace.

-13-

Tasha dashed beyond the reach of the advancing Sage. She saw the determined look in Emeralda's eyes, a look that pierced her deeply, filling her with apprehension. Now, she stood dumbfounded - Emeralda had collapsed to her knees with Timmy standing over her. What a surprise!

As surprising as that was, Tasha was amazed by the sudden change in Emeralda. The Sage went from a daring, determined attack to a complete collapse - seemingly unable to respond. Tasha watched, fascinated by the change in circumstances. However, she was wary that this might only be an act by a clever opponent.

Emeralda closed her eyes as she endured the sudden change of events. A continuous flow of shock passed through her body. She was unable to speak or even moan; she had never experienced a sensation like this, which took away all control of voluntary movement. It coursed through her brain as sharp painful pulses. She could only hope that it would soon end.

The sudden change surprised Timmy too. One moment Emeralda attacked them and the next she was on her knees without energy. *What's going on? I can't tell if she's faking; it doesn't feel like she is. Why would she?* He couldn't risk releasing Emeralda for fear of her quick responses. He was unable to see her face since she had fallen to her knees with her head drooped downward. *I have to talk to her.*

"Emeralda, you must say it; you must cooperate and promise not to try that touch spell again."

He waited for a response but none was forthcoming. Unwilling to take a chance Timmy didn't let her go.

Emeralda wanted Timmy to release her - she had never before experienced such painful sensations. She could hear him asking but couldn't respond. She couldn't even get out a grunt. *How's he able to do this? Just make it go away. I'm in agony.*

Tasha circled around the pair watching Emeralda very carefully. Emeralda's face showed the agony she was feeling. As she moved closer, the Sage didn't react. Tasha was positive that this wasn't an act. Tasha looked at Timmy. "You must let her go. She's lost all control and is in deep pain. I don't understand what you're doing but she's really suffering. She can't take much more."

Timmy heard Tasha's plea; he thought it unusual since she had suffered so much at the hands of Emeralda. *I can't stand here forever holding Emeralda by the wrists; my attempts to talk to her haven't gone anywhere. Just maybe it's like Tasha said: Emeralda's unable to reply. What now?*

If this is just an act then releasing Emeralda might be their last moments of freedom. If it were a fact then freeing her would be a generous, uncalled act of kindness and might lead to further cooperation. It really wasn't that difficult for Timmy to decide. He remembered the golden rule; it was clear what he had to do. He opened his grip on Emeralda's wrists and stepped back.

Emeralda was suddenly aware that the pain was gone. She couldn't understand it. She had no idea how it was possible; as long as Timmy held her wrists she endured pulses of excruciating pain surging through her body, losing all control of movement and voice. Now the pain was gone. Timmy had released her wrists. *Why? Silly boy! You had complete control over me and you let me go. Do I dare to make a move to cast a spell?*

In her weakened state, Emeralda worried that she might not be quick enough and the spell wouldn't be effective. She needed time to regain her strength. She lifted her face and realized that Timmy was still standing before her, looking directly into her eyes.

"Emeralda, I just freed you. Don't forget the pain that you experienced. You don't want to return there."

Emeralda shuddered at the thought.

Timmy continued, "You aren't to cast your spell over us again. It isn't necessary."

"Not necessary! How would you know what's necessary, young prince? You can't know but I do. I didn't mean any harm but you had to accompany me."

"Yes, yes, you said that already. You didn't need to place us under a spell to get us to cooperate. Now things are different and it's you who has to cooperate with us. You have us here and we don't know where here is. We need you, Emeralda, and we're going to help you. You need us obviously because you brought us here; in return you're going to help us."

Emeralda listened closely to Timmy. *He's too reasonable; there has to be a catch somewhere. This isn't the way to get things done.* She had wielded power and used intimidation for so long other methods no longer seemed possible. Yet, a memory of something closely resembling Timmy's version floated just beyond her grasp. Suddenly, it disappeared in a whiff like a puff of smoke. She tried to think of a way to regain her control but she'd have to overcome a formidable foe, one capable of inflicting great pain by simply touching her.

"Emeralda, consider what I've just said. We need you; you need us. It's in our mutual interest to work together, to cooperate so that both of us will achieve our goals. You must promise not to place us under a spell. You must promise to free us and lead us out of Gorn to our home after we've helped you. What do you say?"

Emeralda grunted. She hated being forced to make a decision, but she knew that Timmy was right. *I need Timmy.* She hadn't considered the reciprocal need. Indeed, Tasha and Timmy really did need her. How could she use this to her advantage? Nothing seemed apparent. *He's right. Oh! How I hate to admit that.*

"Young prince, you're so level-headed in your reasoning. You could've gained so much more by holding out. I don't understand why you let me go. You've so much to learn about power and how to use it to your advantage."

"Emeralda, stop right there." Tasha interrupted her. "You're a wonder, you know. Timmy had you completely under his control. Your pain paralyzed you in great agony. Timmy freed you from that torture. Do you show any gratitude? No! Instead, you won't answer that simple question with a simple yes; instead, you start talking about exercising power. Shame on you."

Emeralda stared at Tasha. She was incensed that this girl interrupted her. *You're just a young, untalented girl rebuking me. Yet, there's something about you that I now see that I haven't observed before. Sure, I captured you to serve as bait. Now, I wonder at what hidden strengths you have; you completely fooled me into believing you were hurt. Shame, indeed! How dare you.* Yet again, a memory poked her consciousness. She couldn't make it out. It just sat there nagging her like the name of someone you know but you cannot bring it to mind. She sensed that it was a pleasant memory from her past. Oh, she wished she could grasp it firmly but again it slipped away.

Emeralda glared at Tasha defiantly. Tasha remained locked in her stare and after a moment Emeralda dropped her eyes and her head.

"Young prince, I bow before you. You've shown that you are different. I don't know where your power comes from or why you choose to use it as you do. This girl rebuked me for not showing gratitude. I am grateful you released me from that painful paralysis. You were kind to an old woman to release her." *Why am I taking all the blame?* "You were very cruel to cause this poor old woman such agony but you did show kindness in letting me go. For that I thank you."

Tasha was shocked. Emeralda actually said thank you but what a witch! She blames Timmy for the whole thing.

"I don't believe this." Tasha turned away in annoyance.

Timmy stepped back from Emeralda, laughing. "You're welcome. You still don't get it, do you Emeralda?"

Emeralda raised her head and stared at Timmy. What's he laughing about? I don't see anything funny in what's happened. How can such a powerful prince relax and laugh in a serious circumstance such as this.

"Prince, you mock me now that you've shown your strength"

"No, Emeralda. I don't mock you. I know you're a powerful Sage. I find your blaming me for your pain humourous since it was your actions that brought all this on. We were comfortably having our lunch when you attacked us. You brought this on yourself." Timmy shook his head; all of this seemed lost on Emeralda who was downcast.

Emeralda pondered what Timmy had said. Memories of joy and happy times kept bumping the fringes of her mind but when she tried to recall them, they simply disappeared - much to her dismay. *I want his help and now have to choose. I hate choices.* Emeralda was accustomed to simply acting as she saw fit. This situation placed the future beyond her sole control and she dreaded the uncertainty of it.

Emeralda sighed, knowing she was beaten. She looked up at the young people. "You have me now. I can see that I must go along with you. I believe my way would have been quicker and more effective but since you're now in control, I'll surrender to your wishes. What do we do next?"

Timmy grinned. "Still on that kick, Emeralda. No matter, if you cooperate with us, we'll do the same for you. But you still haven't come through with what's required to start this entire arrangement."

Emeralda looked baffled, glancing at Timmy and then turning towards Tasha. "I said I surrender- what else is there? Give me my instructions."

Tasha shook her head, "Emeralda, Timmy doesn't need you to surrender. He hasn't any desire to control you as you did with us. Don't you see that? He wants you to act on your honour."

Emeralda turned to Timmy with a puzzled look. "I don't get it. What do you want?"

Timmy admired Tasha's cool approach to things and her comprehension of what he wanted. He turned and looked Emeralda in the eyes. "You aren't a slave. You aren't a captive. You're free but if you want our help, you must promise not to harm us or to put us under a spell. When we've helped you, then you'll take us home. We need this promise and we need it now." *This is just a bluff; if Emeralda refuses, we don't have a backup plan. We need her if we're to get back. I have no idea where we are – we can't simply walk away from Emeralda. Besides, I have to look after Tasha - she's here because of me.*

Emeralda groaned at the prospect of making a promise. I haven't made a pledge since touching the lodestone. She cringed at the thought of making a promise. I'm a Sage; I've been trained as a promise keeper - a promise leaves me no choice. She glared at the young man who refused to be intimidated by the venom in her eyes. There's no way out of this dilemma. She could not see the bluff in front of her because she only saw her plans slipping away if Timmy refused to help her. Maybe, I can still get what I want even if I promise. Yes, that's the only way.

"Okay, dear prince, I'll do as you ask. Since you don't give me any choice, I'll promise what you ask. I won't harm you, I won't place you under a spell and I will lead you home. There, you have what you want. You know a promise made by a Sage must be carried out so now you can count on this," Emeralda said softly.

Timmy looked up at Tasha. Both were shocked at this revelation and pleased with the promise. Then they both smiled.

-14-

Emeralda looked at the two smiling young people and wondered aloud, "So what do we do now?"

Timmy motioned to the rest area, "Let's sit down and talk about this."

Tasha moved over to a sitting log. Timmy found one to the right of Tasha and made himself comfortable. Emeralda remained on her knees, watching the other two. She watched Tasha and Timmy sit down. *Just like that. That's all there's to it.*

She stood up at once and, not wanting to be the slow one, made her way to a third log to the right of Timmy. She stood there a moment half considering her next move and then sat down facing Tasha.

"We're on a mission to protect the lodestone." I can't tell them I wish to steal it. I have to make up some story to cover the real reason for taking the stone.

"Before you interrupt me, let me tell you why this needs to be done. A maniac has been following me for a long time, a tyrant far worse than Gorn's ever seen. He's capable of inflicting more suffering than anyone has ever experienced and he does so for no other reason than he's able to. Through my circle of trusted informants, I've discovered that he wants to steal the lodestone, the principal defence of Gorn. He apparently has devised a plan to steal it and then turn its force against Gorn. This can't be allowed to happen."

Emeralda paused for a moment. “Sure, you look at me with distrust and I deserve some of it. It’s true that I’ve long wanted to gain control of it. In fact, I had it in my possession for sometime when it needed protection, I had guarded it for three cycles and then it called out to me to save it from the enemy. I did that and what thanks did I get. The Council accused me of stealing it; the Sages took the stone from me leaving me in a wretched state. Not only that, I was brutally imprisoned. Later, after I was free, I continued to hear the stone calling out to me. I’m unable to go to it because it’s locked away but I must try. If the enemy seizes it before we can get there we’re all doomed.”

Timmy looked at Tasha who rolled her eyes confirming she felt much the same as he did. Timmy recalled the story of Emeralda and the stone. The Sage had been seriously injured trying to take the stone. He knew Emeralda enlisted the help of Ebony, a princess from his homeland, who then stole the stone for her and how they used it to maintain a small kingdom until Ebony had grown old and feeble. Emeralda found another princess who was injured by the stone when she took it from its pedestal. After Emeralda left the injured princess in a miserable state, Marlen found the princess. He nursed her back to health with the help of a newly found prince. Marlen trained the two and then the trio wrested the stone away from Emeralda and Ebony, returning it to the Sages.

The Sages imprisoned Emeralda and Ebony together until Ebony died. Shortly after that, Emeralda escaped and continued to seek a way of regaining the lodestone. *Her explanation is full of lies and distortions but this new enemy really bothers me. I know the enemy wants the stone. What if he has a plan to steal it? We must prevent that.*

"Emeralda, I think you still want the stone for yourself. The desire to possess it drives you. We'll not help you get it for yourself. However, we can't let this tyrant take it either. Who is this enemy? Is it Chrane himself?"

Emeralda cackled at the sound of that name. "Oh how I wish it was Chrane but Chrane's a nobody now. Sure, Chrane was leader of the dark forces but when he allowed the Sages to regain control of the dark lands, let Marlen escape from prison, and permitted his commander to be defeated by that little girl, Chrane's days were over. He was punished. The chief of all the dark forces, Natas, took his place. Now there's a foe! He's a ruthless, single-minded enemy. He can breathe fire; he can burn you up with a single horrifying glance. Natas wants to place all of Gorn under his control before it's too late. Believe me, we must stop him."

Timmy stood up and paced back and forth. I never expected to hear about a new enemy. Chrane was bad enough but now there are dark forces far more powerful. As hard as it is to rely on Emeralda for information, we have to prevent this new Natas from gaining the stone. That is, if he exists – but can we take the chance that he doesn't.

Timmy looked to Tasha for some support since she was watching both of them. Tasha had listened to the story that Emeralda told and to Timmy's response to it. She had no idea who Chrane or Natas might be except that they were very dangerous and evil. *I'm skeptical of Emeralda's story. Could it be that there is no Natas at all and that the supposed danger is only a ruse by Emeralda? How can I communicate my doubts to Timmy? Chrane, I realize, is real since Timmy has mentioned him before Emeralda did.* Tasha shrugged her shoulders. She needed to learn so much about this place. *Maybe, I need to push her and try to discover more.*

Tasha turned to her foe. "Emeralda, I find your story a bit too loose, even for someone as ill-informed as I am. Why should we believe you? You captured us; you kept us drugged, unable to move or talk; you have tried to recapture us. How do we know there's someone following you or how dangerous he might be? You've shown that you're incapable of trust. Why trust you now? How do we know you have a group of spies like you said? The rotten way you treat people makes me wonder if any one would want to be an informant for you. You say the lodestone's crying out for you. I doubt it. It's more likely that you're crying out for it since it was taken away from you. You're so consumed by it that you want it back at any cost."

Emeralda cringed as Tasha tore her story apart; her rage welled up inside her. You have some nerve. You don't have any talents; you were just a random grab as bait and now you're calling a great Sage a liar. Her anger coloured her a deep red as she clenched her fists. She rose from her seat uttering guttural grunts and shrieks.

Timmy was immediately to his feet facing her as he suddenly worried that the promise was about to be broken. *This is amazing - Tasha has shown nerve in standing up to Emeralda.*

Emeralda glared and shrieked at Tasha, "You're an ignorant, noisy, little brat. You have no idea what happens here and yet you think that you can interfere in matters way beyond your understanding. Stay out of things that are none of your business."

Emeralda and Tasha locked in defiant glares. Tasha had no intention of backing down and any fear she had previously was now replaced by smoldering anger. *Brat indeed, I've some choice terms for you.*

Timmy shook his head. *This could get nasty.* "Emeralda, you're wrong in saying Tasha has no business in this. You gave her the right to be involved by kidnapping and bringing her here. It's all your doing. She's as involved as I am - never forget that. Now sit down; let's discuss this calmly. How do you answer the concerns that Tasha raised? I'd like to know more. So, some maniac is chasing you. What about this obsession of yours for the lodestone. I'm wondering if this is another attempt to gain control over it for yourself."

Emeralda and Tasha sat down. Emeralda continued to glare at Tasha with a look that could curdle milk but Tasha was not about to be cowed by that. She was determined to find out what the old witch was up to, except she had other words to describe her. Both remained tense.

Emeralda was amazed at how these two young people knew so much about her – it was almost as if they could read her mind. *Maybe, that was it. Maybe that's the secret of their powers - they can mindlink.*

That didn't make any sense. She had lots of experience with mindlinks and they were always two-way means of communicating. She didn't open the mindlink for fear of the other Sages making contact with her. She didn't sense any probing, the usual indication that a mindlink was occurring. *They are uncanny in their perception and they seem to agree with each other without talking. They must to be able to read my mind and communicate with each other without talking. This is going to be difficult. If I change my story - if they can read my mind... what do I do?'*

Timmy looked at her. "Well, how about it? What are you going to tell us? Now be careful, don't go changing your story because we're listening carefully to every word."

Emeralda shuddered and began with a whimper. "What chance does a poor old woman have when young people surround her and force her to behave the way they want?"

"Nonsense, sheer nonsense!" Timmy declared as he sat down. "You're not a helpless old woman. You're completely in control of yourself. We're here because you brought us here. We had no choice in that. We have to rely on you to take us home and you have promised to do that. We've agreed to help you but it'd better be legitimate. Don't go lying to us leading us into adventures of trouble. We need straight talk. You said you guarded the stone and that indeed is true. You came under its spell because you were left too long with it. Too long! All the Sages know that and all regret leaving you there. You had to endure a terrible burden during that time but now you do nothing to improve its after-effects. Just know this: we won't help you take the stone for yourself and we aren't going to tolerate any more lies and self pity."

Emeralda cringed at his voice. She had lost and she knew she had to cooperate. *I might be able to use this time to formulate a plan to still get what I want.*

"Dear prince, I won't lie to you. I am being pursued by Natas; the longer we stay here, the more likely he's to find us. We must press on. I shudder at the thought of being captured by him. You should be fearful too. I'm dreadfully afraid that he will steal the lodestone - through it he'll dramatically increase his power over Gorn. But don't worry; I believe we can thwart his efforts by checking on the force field around the stone. If it's defective we should move it to a safer place."

Timmy listened carefully to Emeralda. She remained true to her story and did not expand or explain any of the inconsistencies. Nor did she react to Timmy's recount of her time with the lodestone. She avoided the issues raised by

Tasha. *I will have to do some fancy maneuvering to get more out of her.*

“Emeralda, I suppose you have a safer place already arranged. Why don’t you go the Sages with your information? They could find a secure place or increase the existing security around the lodestone.”

Emeralda jumped to her feet, which caused both Timmy and Tasha to stand up. “I can’t go to them. They hate me. Look at what they’ve done to me. They’d either laugh at me or lock me up like they did before and then hide away the stone so that I could never….”

She caught herself and sobbed. “They would hide the stone and I’d never see it again. You must know how devastating that would be to me. That stone’s like a child to me. I could never bear to have it taken completely away by either Natas or the Sages. Please, young prince, you must help me save my little one.”

Timmy sat back down and inhaled a large breath of air. Both Tasha and Emeralda slowly sat down. Timmy looked over to Tasha who pursed her lips and exhaled slowly through them. *Wow!* No other thought went through their minds. He got up and walked around the rest area for a few minutes. Emeralda continued to sit with her head down sobbing and moaning. Tasha rose and came to his side and they moved farther from the sobbing woman to be out of earshot.

“What do you think?” Tasha asked.

“Well, I believe her last statement to be the closest to the truth. She had a terrible experience with the lodestone and it continues to play on her mind in ways that we’ll never know. It’s like a child to her. Notice how she caught herself.”

"Yes I did. She was going to say something about what she wouldn't be able to do without the stone if it were hidden away. She then changed her story slightly."

"Yes, Tasha, she's deathly afraid that the lodestone might be put so far away that she could never see it again. As long as it's held in the force field, she at least knows where it is. If it's removed, she will be absolutely lost. Wow! She's in a dreadful state."

Tasha sneered. "Well she has it coming! What an evil person! Maybe, it should be hidden away somewhere."

"Tasha, Tasha, where's that sympathetic girl who a short time ago pleaded with me to release her? Could you be just a little upset about being called a brat? Now, really, Tasha! You did a marvellous job on her. You've convinced her that your injury was just an act and that really has her baffled. Then you tore apart her story and she really blew. Don't get uptight with her reaction now, just when I need you. Yes, she's evil; she's suffering; she's a liar and she's pathetic. You showed your true self back there. Don't demean yourself because of her."

Tasha looked at Timmy and grinned. "Yes, I admit she got to me. Well, now what? Don't worry about me. This brat can take it."

They both laughed and turned to Emeralda. She looked up at them. "Why did you do it? You had me firmly under your control and in pain. Why did you let me go? I don't understand."

Timmy and Tasha both started to laugh again. Emeralda just sat there bewildered.

Tasha said, "No, you just don't understand."

They continued to laugh, even to howl, at the confused look on Emeralda's face.

-15-

Suzy was enthralled with the sight of the Palace as they moved towards the entry gate. Its walls were ornately sculpted with statuettes and friezes arranged around mirror-like windows which reflected the light in a scatter pattern producing fascinating colours and giving a jewel-like appearance to the entire structure. *I have never, in all my life, seen any building so beautiful.* Suzy remembered another city that she had studied descending to earth from the clouds in the book called Revelation. She was happy her friends were with her because they kept her moving. She could've just stood there in awe at the incredible majesty of the palace.

Marlen and Sapphira didn't intend to leave her in rapt wonder. They proceeded through the open gateway and into the spacious courtyard. The wide-open area to the left was occupied by a caravan of merchants who had set up a bazaar and were selling their wares from tables, out of booths and off curtains. The field to the right was abuzz with soldiers performing maneuvers and training in small groups under the instruction of their officers. Suzy stopped to gaze in fascination at the skilled movements with which the small cohorts performed. They advanced with intricate timing and turned with precision.

"So much of this is your doing." Marlen interrupted her thoughts. "We now have soldiers who are dedicated to excellence, discipline and a determination not to allow the darkness to return this land. They have proven themselves in many skirmishes and have engaged with the dark forces, every time driving back the enemy and securing the borders. They, indeed, have proven their worth and bravery."

"I can't take credit for any of this. This all happened since I was here last."

"True, but it was the work of the two of you that got it all started. When Timmy healed a poor old soldier and when the two of you rescued him from the prison, you had no idea what forces you unleashed in Gorn. That simple soldier has become the undisputed and highly admired commander of all the troops in this land. Blog has dedicated himself to the service of his land and the welfare of his companions and fellowmen. He is an inspiration to all around him."

Suzy beamed at the mention of her simple soldier friend. Blog had cringed in that prison cell so afraid of the dark. He took command after the attacks showing great bravery and loyalty. It was wonderful to hear how he had advanced, discovering hidden talents, stepping forward to take control of his life and affecting all those around him.

"Where is he? I really want to see him."

"Patience, little one," Sapphira advised quietly. "He's supervising his troops as they complete their daily drills. Let's walk over to that raised viewing stand where they provide benches so that anyone can observe the movements and drills."

They walked over to the platform prepared for spectators. They climbed the stairs; the Sages found seats for themselves. Suzy remained standing with her hands resting on the rail, totally engaged in the performance before her on the grounds. Several groups of soldiers were advancing with swords drawn and shields held high. They moved in-step and advanced as a single unit. They would step forward, then slide to the left, advance several steps, drop their shields and turn as a group to the right followed by more advancing. Another group was performing a pike attack. Advancing and turning with pikes involves great timing and patience. It had the appearance of a wall of spikes suddenly converting into a cushion of upwardly lifted needles turning gently then the wall reappearing in another direction. The choreography involved in this special dance fascinated Suzy.

Some groups were practising one-on-one duelling with either swords or maces; others were engaged in hand-to-hand combat.

Suzy scanned the entire field, spending a few seconds enjoying the spectacle then moving on to the next display. As much as she enjoyed each drill, her mind was elsewhere as she searched for her friend on the field. *There are so many soldiers milling about, I can't spot Blog at all.*

Suddenly, near the middle of the field about one hundred paces from her stand Suzy spotted a soldier waving to her. She jumped up and down, frantically waving as she bubbled with excitement. Blog made his way through the field of active soldiers deliberately maneuvering so as not to interfere with the drills. He continued to wave his hand. Suzy turned to her friends who nodded their approval. She made her way to the head of the stairs that led to the field.

Sapphira spoke as Suzy prepared to descend the stairs, "Just to the bottom step, my dear. Please stay off the field."

"Thanks."

She descended the stairs to the lowest step where she waited for her friend who was now free of the groups of men and was striding quickly across the open area towards the stand. He was smiling broadly. Suzy could hardly contain herself, fighting back the urge to dash forward but she remained mindful of what her wise friend had just told her.

When Blog came quite near he suddenly went down on both knees and bowed deeply to her. "Dear princess, I'm so happy to see you. What an honour you bestow on me by coming out to watch our drill. I bow before you in gratitude and reverence…."

Suzy left her step and walked directly over to the kneeling soldier. She placed her hand on his shoulder and placed the other hand over his mouth. "Please stand up, dear Blog. Get up off your knees. Do not bow before me on your knees. You do me a great honour but I don't deserve this and I can't have you kneeling in reverence before me."

"But my dear princess. You and the prince rescued me from a life of darkness and nothingness. I'm so grateful to you as lords…."

"Stop it now, Blog. Please get up. There's only one Lord and I too bow before Him. So does Timmy. You can't do that to me. Stand up, dear friend."

Blog slowly got to his feet, visibly upset and confused. "Dearest princess, I don't understand. All my life I've bowed to those in power over me. You're my saviour and I wish to do the same."

Suzy took Blog's hand in hers. "There's only one Saviour, dear Blog. I'm a friend only; it's out this friendship that I ask you not to pay homage to me. I'm honoured by your gratitude and happy to see you again."

Blog smiled and turned towards the field. "These troops are under my command. They've been waiting for the time when they too could display their reverence to you. They wish to come forward and bow in submission to you."

"They can not, I won't let them. I'm but a young girl. Instead. I'll let them march by as I review their groups. There'll be no bowing or kneeling."

Blog nodded. "I'll arrange a march past. They'll be so pleased to do this for their princess. They consider you their commanding officer."

Suzy laughed at this news. "Really Blog! How can a young girl command such a well-trained group of soldiers? I'm tickled, of course. I'll be thrilled to meet with you after to talk about all that's happened."

Blog smiled at Suzy's invitation following which he set off across the field to arrange for the march by. Suzy climbed the stairs to return to her friends. They both nodded to her.

Marlen spoke softly, "Well done, my young friend. You've shown great wisdom. I'm so pleased that you refused to allow Blog to continue. There's much about you that's beyond our understanding; you surprise us with your beautiful behaviour."

"Thanks Marlen, it's really easy when you have love in your heart. Any action's easy then."

-16-

Blog came walking across the field to meet Suzy after the march by - Suzy had stood on the viewing stand watching the soldiers pass by. They proudly displayed their training and discipline and after completing their demonstration, they stood at attention before the stand as Suzy waved to them. They removed their headpieces and shouted exuberantly, "Hail Princess, dear friend." She held up her hand to stop them; they continued shouting, "Princess, princess." After several moments of this and what seemed an eternity for Suzy, Blog called them to attention and they marched away in order and in quickstep. Suzy felt deeply honoured by their show of respect and gratitude.

Sapphira and Marlen took their leave after the march so that Suzy could have some private time with her friend. Suzy waited for Blog by sitting on the bench on the viewing stand. She closed her eyes and dozed for a short time, feeling tired after the long journey to the palace.

She rose to her feet when she saw Blog walking across the field towards her. Now she waited for her friend as he approached with a big smile on his face. He reached the base of the stand and began to ascend the steps, one at a time, with a measured pace. When he reached the top Suzy ran to him and gave him a big hug. Blog responded with a bear hug and turned her around once before setting her back down on her feet. He stepped back and grinned.

"Oh, it's so good to see you, Princess. My! How you've grown."

"Blog, it's good to be here again with you. Your soldiers are simply amazing. You've trained them well; I can see they're ready for any combat that comes their way. That march by was incredible - I was deeply moved by their shouts of appreciation."

Blog grinned, "They'll be pleased when I tell them. It was an incredible performance by a group of incredible soldiers. They're well prepared to serve in the defence of Gorn. It probably comes from having been subjects of darkness; they now want to keep the light shining in the world."

"Blog, you're too modest. They're totally devoted to you and would follow you to the ends of the world."

Blog cleared his throat. "Princess, I think you exaggerate my importance. These men are patriotic; they're well trained; they're prepared to fight any dark force. Of course, so am I. I'd go the end of the world to do so."

Suzy sat down and patted the bench beside her. Blog hesitated a moment and after Suzy smiled he sat down next to her. Suzy continued to smile.

"Friend, I want to hear about what you've been doing since I was here last. You seem to have been very busy and quite successful as well."

"A great deal's happened and although my time's been very full I've never been happier. Before I met the two of you, I really didn't know what happiness was. I'd gone from one job to another and finally been trapped by that dark captain who promised so much to his soldiers but never delivered on anything, except a constant and relentless demand for absolute obedience. Fear was the only reward we received;

fear guaranteed that we'd never act in a contrary fashion. The day the darkness descended on our land was the beginning of a nightmare of terror and blindness. We were forced to remember our way by touch and feel. The only way out was to follow that stream so we were always wet and cold. Being in the darkness gave us some protection because our mistakes couldn't be seen but the comfort was false because that captain often produced a light, which found us out. When we did go beyond the dark curtain in the world of light we were always apprehensive of being watched - most of us found relief by returning." Blog stopped, taking a deep breath since he was rapidly inhaling and exhaling.

"Dear Blog! That must've been awful! I can't imagine how bad it was to be in darkness all the time."

"Awful sort of describes it. I remember the day when we came across some tracks leading into the curtain and how I was drawn to be the one to find out who was there. True, they tied a rope around me but I'd no experience with that location. You can't even imagine how frightening that was. I was terrified of a strange light; I was wounded and after I was pulled out, my companions jeered and left me in that injured state, running off to tell the captain. After I passed out because I lost so much blood, I could have died. I was frightened when I came to with someone's hands pressed down on me. I bolted up the stream and cared not what awaited me. I just had to get away. The captain wanted to know how I could still be alive because my companions said they had left me for dead. When I couldn't explain it, my commander was furious with all of us but especially with me. I was thrown into prison. Timmy and you found and freed me because you said it was the right thing to do. I have since tried to live my life like that, dear princess, for others and not for myself. When my companions came out and heard my story they wanted to do the same. All the soldiers who followed me desired the same type of life. Since then our numbers have grown. I want the best for them and I won't make promises to them that I don't intend to keep. We're your soldiers, dear princess. You've shown us a new way."

Suzy was amazed and pleased to hear how Blog had turned his life around. She put her hand on his shoulder and gave it a gentle squeeze. "Well done, friend. I can see how far you've come."

"Why have you returned, dear princess? What matter of urgency brought you back?"

"Oh, Blog, it's Emeralda again."

At the name of that foe Blog's face took on a very concerned look, "Her again! What's she done now?"

"She's captured Timmy. I'm not certain how she did it but I think she used another girl disguised as me to lure Timmy into a trap. I was following them but they crossed over into Gorn and I was unable to follow. I found a gateway and began a search in Gorn. Sapphira found and brought me here. I've no idea where they are and neither do the Sages."

Blog jumped to his feet and began to pace back and forth, pounding his right fist into his left hand. "We need to find them but Gorn's a large place - they could be anywhere. We'll need to send out word about this. If anyone sees them, it'll be reported back to us. The good thing is that Timmy's a very capable prince who can look after himself. Still, Emeralda's a terrible companion with so much power at her command."

"It really is amazing how I keep hearing that same thing said about Timmy over and over again. I too know it to be true. It makes me feel so much better."

Blog resumed his seat and turned to Suzy. "Okay, I have told you about myself. What about yourself?

Suzy smiled, "Well I don't have much to tell you and certainly not as exciting. I've continued to help out on my parent's farm."

"You also have grown since you were here."

"That's true. My clothes have become too small but I can now reach places that before were too high."

They chuckled and then Blog became very serious, "I need to know why you refused to let me kneel before. Timmy and you are my lords. I've decided to serve you in thanks for what you did for me. If I'm unable to do this I'll be as lost as I was in the dark."

"Blog, I appreciate what you're saying, believe me, but I can't ask you to serve me in that manner. I didn't do anything except what's expected of me. It pleases me to see you wish to do the same."

"Princess, whom do you serve? You said you have a lord. Why won't you be mine? You saved me; I owe it to you as my…." Blog paused, remembering Suzy's powerful talk. "Who is your Saviour?"

"Dear Blog, you're obviously ready for so much more. Do you read?"

"Yes princess, I was trained in the art of reading; it's very useful in sending and receiving messages."

Suzy reached into the backpack sitting on the bench. She took out a black covered book and set it on her lap. "Blog, here I've the most powerful and beautiful message ever written. In this book is the story of the true Saviour, the one that both Timmy and I serve. I'm going to take this time to tell you the most wonderful story that has ever been told."

-17-

After Tasha and Timmy finished their good laugh, they asked Emeralda to lead them onward. They quickly packed and boarded the wagon while Emeralda took the reins and urged the horse down the road. They continued until they crossed a bridge over a fast moving brook in which they saw shiny rainbow trout leaping in the flashing water. They turned left just past the bridge and followed a less used road, which snaked along the bank of this stream.

After several hours, they stopped to rest the horse and to prepare a meal for themselves. Timmy and Tasha were amazed at how efficiently their host took over this task and put a delicious meal of hot cakes and sausages before them. She insisted that they should care for the horse and fill the water buckets. After this quick meal, they cleaned their bowls and utensils, packed them up and continued on their way.

This time Timmy and Tasha chose to sit at the back of the wagon with their legs dangling over the end and they quietly went over everything that had happened and tried to map out a strategy. They, at least, felt more comfortable with each other although they really had no idea what was about to happen. Timmy found out that Tasha was from a small village several miles from where he lived. She was his age and in the same grade. “I don’t know why I was so stupid as to let Emeralda capture me. I’ve been taught to avoid strangers.”

Timmy put his index finger to his lips. "Sshh! Emeralda still thinks you faked your injury. Let's keep it that way." Timmy spoke in a whisper.

Tasha nodded. "What's Gorn like? So far, all I've seen is open countryside. Some is very beautiful but it's so empty."

"Most people live in villages for protection. The dark forces have run over the land so many times that people refuse to live by themselves."

"We haven't seen anyone. What are they like, people of Gorn. Are they gnomes or some other strange creatures?"

Timmy laughed. "What an imagination you have? You've met Emeralda; she's a Sage. There are other Sages, much like her."

"Oh, no. There are more like her."

Emeralda looked over her shoulder and glared at Tasha. Tasha missed the look but Timmy caught it. He lowered his voice. "I've only met two others. Marlen is a kind, elderly man who is also the head of the Sage Council. Sapphira is Emeralda's sister and is as different as day is from night. Sapphira was our guide during our adventure into Gorn. The other people in Gorn are much like us, except there are fewer and they don't get old very quickly. There are also very few children."

"They don't die?"

"Very few – Sages have healing powers as do some of the dark commanders. However, we saw a soldier who was cut down and died of his wounds because no one came to heal him."

"So Gorn is different than home. I'll try to get used to it."

As the day ended, they parked the wagon near the stream and in the shelter of a bluff of trees. They ate a cold meal and prepared for night. Emeralda produced sleeping gear from a compartment under the seat on the wagon, enough for each of them and they found spots around the fire. Timmy added several logs to the fire, which would burn slowly throughout the night. Tasha collapsed into her blankets and fell asleep. Timmy dozed lightly. Emeralda sat watching them, struggling with her desire to rush them and her promise not to harm them. Eventually, she gave up and curled up in her blankets.

Sleep drifted over her like a thick rolling fog. She felt cold, alone, and disturbed at its opaque consistency. She shuddered and slipped into a deeper sleep, forgetting about the presence of the companions who had forced her hand.

Emeralda felt herself falling into an abyss. As she clawed at the sides, her fingers simply passed through something slimy and revolting. Voices cried out to her, taunting her as she continued to descend. Here and there, scenes of light and brilliance would open up to her but before she could clearly make out what they were, they were swallowed up as she sank deeper in darkness.

A cold wind lashed her face numbing her exposed skin. Her fingers were chilled to the bone and her clothing offered little protection from the icy blast. Try as she might to determine whether this flight was real or fantasy her mind refused to cooperate. Suddenly she was no longer falling.

Emeralda was lying on a bed of pebbles and shells that had begun to move beneath her. It was semi-dark around her; above her face swirled an almost impenetrable mist, which allowed only the barest amount of light to pass through. She rose from her marbly bed and groped about. She sensed the presence of some horrible power nearby which both attracted and repulsed her.

The malevolent fog whipped around her, shrieking and moaning. Emeralda felt a stinging sleet lash her face. Something entered her mind, splitting thoughts and warping images. She shuddered and realized she was sitting up staring at the slow burning fire. She continued to shake and breathe rapidly.

She lifted her eyes and found herself staring into the face of Timmy who, propped up on one elbow, was watching her. She dropped her eyes and grunted.

"Are you all right, Emeralda?"

"Why wouldn't I be?" She grunted again and drew her covers over her shoulders, settling into her bed. She opened one eyes slightly to see that Timmy continued to watch her intently. "Just a silly nightmare," she added. *Why did I do that? I don't owe you any explanations; the sooner we complete our task the sooner I can be rid of the two of you.*

Emeralda shuddered again at the fast fading memory of her dream and again stole a peek. Nothing had changed. Timmy continued to watch, almost as though he was guarding the camp. *Silly boy, there are no dangers around here. I've used a search spell to check out the vicinity.* Still, she felt comforted by his soft words and by his presence as she drifted off into a tranquil, deep and relaxing sleep.

-18-

The sound of birds singing joyful tunes brought Timmy out of a deep sleep. He lay for a short, enjoying the sun shining on his covers. As he did, he became aware of other sounds in the camp. He looked around and saw that his companions were awake and preparing the breakfast meal. Emeralda had gathered some wood, had the fire going and had brought some water to heat. Tasha was going through the supplies to find some breakfast materials. Timmy pushed off his covers and stood up. Both women looked his way but only Tasha had anything to say.

"Finally decided to wake up, sleepy head? Well, we're busy preparing so why don't you check on the horse and get ready.

Timmy wandered over to where the horse was grazing and checked it over, softly talking to the animal and stroking its face. The horse nickered and went on grazing. Timmy walked through the small grove of trees and looked out to the east. He could see that the road went on alongside the stream but he could make out a walking bridge that crossed the stream some distance away. Timmy walked down to the stream where he washed up and brushed his hair. *That will have to do.* He climbed the bank to return. Before carrying on, he looked off in the distance to see a blue range of hills. He turned and made his way back into the camp where breakfast was ready.

Each dished up a large bowl of porridge. They ate in silence with Emeralda watching the young people intently. When

Timmy had finished his meal, he set the bowl aside and turned to Emeralda. “So what happens from here, Emeralda? You led us this far. Now, we want to know where we are headed.”

“We are going to the blue mountains in the distance. We’ll be leaving our wagon here and crossing the foot bridge that’s just up stream from here. We’ll take the path that leads up to the hills – we’ll be travelling on foot. It’ll take at least two days, more if you can’t keep up.” Emeralda huffed.

“Don’t worry about us, we’ll keep up and maybe even push you a bit.” Tasha snorted in response to Emeralda. “How will we be able to take all of these supplies?” She pointed around her.

“We’re only taking essentials. A few cooking items, water, food rations, clothing and bedding. We’ll carry some items in our backpacks and in a roll on our lower back. What we don’t take, we’ll store in the wagon until we return. We’ll let the horse roam free. He won’t go far from the wagon.”

“And what will we find in the blue hills, Emeralda,” Timmy asked. “You always seem to leave something out of your explanation.”

“Young prince, I was coming to that before I was interrupted.” Timmy and Tasha both grinned at her. “In a valley in those hills is the castle of the lodestone. We’re going there to make certain that the force field is in place and that Natas hasn’t taken the stone. We can’t delay any longer.”

“But if Natas is somehow following us, aren’t we leading him straight to it? Maybe, we should turn off in a different direction and maybe even go back to our world. That way Natas would be completely misled and the stone would be safe. For all we know Natas could be on the other side of that grove of trees watching and listening to us.” Timmy shrugged.

Emeralda laughed with a cackle. "Always making up stories, young prince. You know what's on the other side of the trees. You were there just a short time ago. No, Natas isn't nearby. I would feel his dreaded presence; besides I've cast a search spell around this area - we're the only people in this vicinity."

"Oh, you're able to do that. We didn't know that you had such a talent," Tasha interrupted.

"There are many things that the two of you don't know. There's much about me that you think you know but you don't."

"I know that you're a mystery but I know some about you from being told and from seeing the way you act," Timmy said. "We could know more if you'd tell us. Isn't that the usual way of finding out information?"

"I'm not your instructor. You say you've been told about me - probably by that meddling old fool, Marlen. Not everything he says is true, you know."

"Well this isn't getting us anywhere. You haven't answered my question. Natas is after you. We know this because you've said so. So if he's following us, why not go elsewhere and lead him astray."

"If only it were that simple, dear boy. Some time ago, I sensed Natas was no longer chasing me. That's worrisome - he's always been after me since I had possession of the lodestone. I can only surmise that he now has new information and begun looking for the stone on his own. If that's the case we must get there before he does."

"And what do we do then?" Tasha asked.

"How do I know?" Emeralda snarled. "I don't know the future. I can't read minds. Why don't the two of you tell me what he's going to do?"

Timmy and Tasha exchanged glances, wondering what Emeralda meant by that. They did not let their bewilderment show since obviously Emeralda was fishing for something.

"Ok, we've finished our meal. What do we do as soon as we've cleaned up this camp?" Timmy asked.

Emeralda shrugged. "I guess we'll pack up what's needed. I'll instruct you in that regard."

Timmy and Tasha stood up and began to wash up the bowls and pots. They rolled up their bedding making a secure small roll for easy carrying. Emeralda busied herself setting out rations that they would take. She gathered up a pot, a kettle and some bowls and spoons, evenly distributing the common items among the three travellers. Each filled a water container and each placed some of the rations and their clothing in the backpacks. Timmy extinguished the fire by pouring water on it. The extra supplies were placed in the storage compartment under the seat on the wagon.

Emeralda removed a package from the storage bin and placed it on the wagon. Timmy and Tasha watched as she unrolled it. From inside the rolled cloth, she produced two scabbards, each holding a short sword. Emeralda handed one to Timmy and the other to Tasha.

"Wear these. We've no idea whether we'll run into some unsavoury characters on this trip or not. Gorn's full of them. You may need to defend yourself."

As Timmy was putting on his, he looked over to Emeralda. What about you? Shouldn't you be carrying a weapon?"

"I've more weapons at my disposal than you know about." Everyone made sure their packs were in place and each checked the others' to make sure that they were secure. Even Emeralda helped with this task, which the young people found a bit unusual but also reassuring. Then they set off walking past the grove of trees and across the grassy plain to the footbridge that crossed the stream. Emeralda took the lead; Tasha followed with Timmy bringing up the rear. He looked back and saw the horse grazing near the grove of trees. He looked abound and listened - nothing seemed to be amiss. He turned, following the others across the bridge and on to the path that led towards the blue hills in the distance. *I wonder what surprises Emeralda has in store for us. Right now, I'd better keep up and concentrate on the journey ahead.*

-19-

It was early morning and Suzy was having breakfast with her companions, enjoying Marlen's storytelling. He filled her in on what had been happening since her last trip to Gorn. The soldiers who had come with Blog had then recruited their comrades after being left leaderless when the dark commander was defeated. Blog relayed the stories of their rescues and the healing at the hands of the prince. None understood why such a wonderful young boy would do such a beautiful thing for them, the enemy. Blog carefully explained how all were brothers and as such, it was a duty to care for all. That simple message combined with the increasing respect for this simple soldier soon had many soldiers joining and dedicating themselves to the service of Gorn under the leadership of Blog. The result was a devoted, well-disciplined army.

Suzy listened as Marlen told her about a new enemy. Chrane was gone, replaced by the leader of the dark forces, Natas, who wanted nothing less than complete control of Gorn. All who stood in his way would be swept away. A new attack was imminent and the Sage army was on the march to prevent it.

Emeralda continued to be a problem for the Sages. She had not done anything major but the Sages used a lot of energy and attention keeping track of her. Emeralda was carefully avoiding the mindlink so they only knew of her whereabouts after the fact. So far, the lodestone had not been disturbed but the Sages knew that was her constant goal.

"We have, of course, the force field around it that's mind linked to all of us. This has freed up a Sage so that no one's physically protecting it as in the past. It's also a guarantee that no one will come under the spell of the stone as Emeralda did. On regular occasions, a Sage goes to the lodestone Castle to physically check on it. The last one to go has returned and all was in order. Emeralda has not been in the vicinity – a spell would tell us if she had been - so we know we're all right for now. That's good because now we have to pay attention to the dark commander."

Suzy looked up at Marlen, "This is when she'll strike. With the Sages busy elsewhere, she'll make her move on the lodestone."

"Very perceptive, young one. Yes, we've thought about that but unfortunately our strength and attention are needed elsewhere. We'll rely on the force field and the fact that Timmy's with her. We're fairly confident that things will work out for the best."

"All right then, what happens next in this campaign against this new dark commander, Natas, you called him?"

Marlen stood up and looked out the window towards the east. "Out there beyond the horizon, armies are on the move. Blog's already left for the frontier taking his crack troops with him. If any troops can put the dark forces to the test it'll be those."

Suzy came and stood beside him. "I wish I could've had more time with him. Marlen, do you know how he clung to every word as I explained the Good News to him. He was so enthralled that he asked for my Bible; I gave it to him. I wish I could be with him."

"Suzy, you've already done so much for that man. Do you realize how blessed all of you believers are? You have a promise and a hope that others can only dream of." Marlen paused. "By the way, Suzy, your wish is about to come true, if you're willing. Sapphira and I want you to accompany us to the frontier."

Wow! They want me to go with them. I know there's danger in going to the front but there's also adventure and intrigue. That will be fascinating.

"Yes, yes, yes! I really want to go with you.... But why do you want me to go with you? I'm not objecting but I know you two all too well. You have a reason for every decision you make."

Sapphira laughed. "Well Marlen, how about that? We can't keep anything from this one."

Sapphira turned to Suzy. "My dear, you're so inquisitive, always seeking out new ideas and not satisfied with just what's before you."

Marlen's eyes twinkled with excitement and pleasure. "Suzy, you're such a dear. We love your straightforwardness and spontaneous responses. Most people suffer because of such quickness but you've a talent for choosing the right time to act. Yes, we want you with us as we go to the frontier. There are dangers involved but I suspect that you already know that.

We'll be very close to the armies of the dark commander and as such are exposed to his strength. However, we feel that we must engage him before he has a chance to recover any of that territory. Sapphira and I feel that your presence with the army will increase our odds for success. The soldiers, who are deeply loyal and highly trained, will respond positively to having their princess with them.

Besides, we know from past experience you're the wielder of hidden power - we may need your strength in this combat."

Suzy turned to her companions and hesitated as she pondered her next question. She indeed was curious and always wanted to know how things worked. "I know I've been involved in some interesting events in the past. What I fail to understand is how I come to have the hidden power to which you refer. I've always considered it just a coincidence that I found that necklace so long ago. All my power, as you call it, comes from that necklace and not from anything special about me. I used the necklace to free the Sages, then to overcome the dark lands, and to defeat the commander. Anyone could have done that if they had the crystals."

Sapphira shook her head. "No, Suzy, that's where you're mistaken. None of us would even attempt to take hold of the crystals, not that we could. You saw what happened to the dark commander when their power was unleashed against him. We're unable to use these tokens because they're not meant for us; they'd be dangerous to our wellbeing."

"Why's that? They have no effect on me…. Well I do hear them at home whenever something's about to happen in Gorn. Oh yes, one of the jewels felt warm to the touch but the others did not. But surely. others would notice these effects as well."

"Have your parents heard the crystals singing to you in the house?" Marlen asked.

Suzy paused for a moment, "I suppose they didn't hear it. Maybe, I got to them quickly enough to silence them before my parents could hear them."

"Really, Suzy!" Marlen exclaimed. "Your mother's able to hear your movements around the house and probably has come to you in the middle of the night when you've been sick or having bad dreams - you don't think she'd hear the chimes, if she could. No, she hasn't been able to hear them because they were meant for your ears only."

Suzy looked down for a moment acknowledging the truth of Marlen's statement. Everything you said about my mother's true. Mom even heard the squeaking of the chipmunk that I hid away in a box at the bottom of my closet. Mom can hear Dad feeding the animals down by the barn from inside her kitchen.

Marlen continued, "Moreover, do you remember I refused to take that ear stud that you found after Emeralda lost it in the field? I didn't take it from you even when you offered it to me. I can't use it - even touching it could be dangerous to me."

Suzy remembered the day when Emeralda had chased her after refusing to follow her to the castle on the plain. I encountered Marlen twice that day, the second time on the road to my home; his presence frightened Emeralda away, but not before the ear stud fell in the field. I saw it fall and ran out to get it. Marlen provided a gold chain so I could wear it around my neck.

"I still have it. In fact, I'm wearing it now because I took it with on this trip."

"Keep it hidden." Sapphira placed a hand on Suzy's shoulder. "It isn't wise to display those items in these dangerous times."

"Why couldn't you handle it, Marlen. After all, you're a Sage; it came from Emeralda who's also a Sage. Surely you wouldn't be in any danger from such an item." Suzy looked at Marlen.

Marlen took both of Suzy's hands in his, "I know these things are hard to understand but please believe me when I say that stud would be dangerous to me and, for that matter also to Sapphira or Blog or anyone from Gorn. It isn't originally from Gorn but belonged to the evil dark lord. He gave it to Emeralda at some point in the past; its purpose remains hidden from us.

Somehow, Emeralda was protected from any harm and you seem to be unaffected by its power."

Suzy shuddered as she recalled the memory of her encounter with the bracelet that Timmy had found. "I guess this is true for many things here in Gorn. I was injured seriously by Timmy's bracelet when I put it on but it has a very different effect for Timmy. Ebony and the earlier prince and princess were able to handle the lodestone which had caused great injury to Emeralda."

"You know all about this." Marlen nodded. "Sometimes understanding what you already know can be very difficult. In fact, there are many things we, as Sages, don't understand even though we've known about them for centuries. I have one correction for you about your recollection; the stone did injure the earlier princess. A word of caution, my dear; be very careful to whom you repeat this information. The enemy has spies everywhere; he even has devised special means to gather information in the most unlikely places."

Sapphira took Suzy's hands in hers. "Suzy, we have discovered that there are young people in your world who, for whatever reason, have hidden talents and strengths that allow them to do things in Gorn that are forbidden to our people. We have known this for centuries but we didn't permit the entry of these princes and princesses into Gorn because this place can be very dangerous; we felt their presence here would disturb the natural balance. Emeralda changed all that when she went searching for a princess, found Ebony, and brought her here. We discovered these young people can do more than handle forbidden objects; they often have hidden strengths that manifest themselves here in Gorn." Sapphira let go of Suzy's hands.

"That would be like Timmy's ability to heal. He has no idea how it works, just that it does and it has worked every time that he has needed it."

"That's correct," Marlen said. "He has healing talents and, as time passes, he's likely to discover that power will display itself in different ways. He definitely has the right attitude for a healer; he's willing to help anyone in need, no matter what they've done in the past."

"That certainly describes Timmy. He's always been kind and gentle. As he's grown older, those traits have matured and displayed themselves more often and in greater degrees. Since we started studying our scriptures more intensively, the fruits of the Spirit have become more evident in him. Perhaps that explains why I don't have any hidden talents like him. I lack the required attitude and bearing that he has."

Marlen took Suzy's hands in his. "Don't be so critical of yourself. Don't sell yourself short. The time hasn't been right for your talents to be revealed. Moreover, you definitely have the talent for bringing the best out in the people with whom you're associated. It's through your work that we now have a strong, well-trained and disciplined army of dedicated soldiers. Just continue to be yourself; that has the greatest impact on all around you." Marlen released Suzy's hands and patted one of them.

Suzy smiled in appreciation of Marlen's kind words. She looked at both her friends. "Thank you for your support. You're the best. Now what happens? Are we ready to go?"

The two Sages laughed. Marlen stopped long enough to say, "Well, well, well! Things are back to normal. We do need some time to put a few travelling items together but, yes, we're almost ready to go."

All three got up and started for the palace to pack their belongings for the journey ahead, still laughing softly.

-20-

Two days later the small caravan moved through a land rich in vegetation that took the form of grasses, ferns, shrubs and widely spaced trees. All the surroundings had a very familiar look to them. Suzy recalled the journey that she took with Sapphira and Timmy as they searched for Marlen. This landscape reminded her of that trip. Now, however, she saw many forms of wildlife. Deer, foxes, gophers and rabbits were scurrying everywhere. The trees rang with the choruses of the many species of birds that nested there. The occasional hawk glided over the land, usually too high to be easily identified, searching for prey too small for normal eyes to see easily. Suddenly, the hunter would go into a rapid dive and pull up just before colliding with ground carrying away in its talons a small rodent or a rabbit that would serve as a meal to a nest full of hungry chicks.

The air was fresh and warm; the sky was a bright blue with an occasional fluffy, white cloud. This was in direct contrast with the cool, dreary, damp journey that she had taken into this region the previous time. She had travelled wet and sullen. Now it was pleasant and enjoyable. Often, Marlen or Sapphira climbed on to her bench on the slow moving wagon to share an interesting conversation with her. Suzy learned that her new enemy was recruiting a fierce army of hill people who had been isolated for a long time due to the dark plague and the centuries-old drought. These unforunates were deeply jealous of their neighbours who seemed to enjoy a profitable, luxurious life in comparison to theirs. It wasn't hard to incite their anger when they were always on the verge of starvation. The enemy's promises of a land of plenty were motivation enough to gain their loyalty.

Sapphira told Suzy that a small region in the adjacent desert had darkened; careful observations revealed the spot was slowly expanding. The Sages believed that this was the dark force's way of establishing a toehold of darkness in Gorn. That small stronghold would expand if the Sages' control waned.

Suzy was enjoying a solitary ride since the last stop for the noontime meal. She carefully took in all the sights around her. She nearly jumped from the wagon in excitement as she spotted a bluff of two trunked trees off to the south. This confirmed her thought that they indeed were nearing the former dark country. As further proof, a small group of soldiers was encamped up the road, waiting for the caravan to arrive. As Suzy watched, three soldiers approached the lead wagon at some distance from the encampment. She realized this was to determine the friendliness of the caravan at a location far enough away from the main body of soldiers. The camp of soldiers wasn't going to be taken by surprise; it also allowed the troops ample time to prepare for the arrival of friends once the identification was made.

The train came to a halt as the soldiers made their way to the first wagon. Suzy could see Marlen step down and walk ahead to greet the commander. The soldiers came to attention and gave him the heart salute. Suzy watched the short conversation that ended with the soldiers again saluting, turning and marching back down the road to their camp. Marlen returned to his wagon and climbed on board but the train didn't start moving immediately.

Suzy took advantage of this stop to scan the scene around her. The grassy plain was interspersed with bluffs of trees, some of which were the double trunked variety. She saw the soldiers had camped near a stream that meandered across the open plain. If this were back home, this land would have been cultivated and supporting fields of cereal or oil-seed crops, gardens of vegetables or orchards of fruit trees. The constant struggle with the dark forces kept the vast fertile countryside of Gorn from producing up to its potential. When darkness had bordered this land, its inhabitants abandoned the land for fear of the dark lord. Even now, that the darkness was gone, there was a reluctance to return to this land for fear that the darkness might come back. It would take time to bring about the healing and the restoration of confidence in the people. The fact that soldiers were on the march through this region would not instill calmness and confidence in the former residents. It was a reminder that the enemy was still a danger and would continue to be until annihilated. People quite properly would not feel safe in this region. According to Marlen, Gorn was about to face one of its greatest tests as Natas attempted to increase his hold over the land. What dangers lay ahead Suzy had no idea but she didn't feel afraid; she had her companions, her loyal soldiers and a strong faith in a saving Lord.

The wagons lurched forward as the train came into motion. Soon, the wagons covered the short distance and drew into a tight circle just outside the camp. Suzy descended from her wagon meeting Sapphira who had come back to find her. Sapphira led her into the encampment. "The soldiers have been waiting for our arrival and have prepared a meal for everyone in the caravan."

Suzy shortly found herself seated at a long mess table and helping herself to a pot of stew consisting mainly of chunks of white meat, beans, onions and white carrot. The aroma was mouth watering; the first spoonful proved how tasty the food was. A plate of biscuits sat on the table; groups of soldiers who kept watch over the table routinely replenished its rapidly dwindling pile. Suzy soon found herself satisfied and pushed her bowl away. "That was absolutely delicious." Sapphira wiped her bowl clean with a part of a biscuit. Suzy took a drink from her cup. The sweet tasting, clear beverage had a hint of cloves. She felt refreshed and energized.

Sapphira turned to her. "That's a great drink after a solid meal. It banishes the usual lethargy that people experience after eating such a good meal. Soldiers particularly like it because it keeps them alert and prepared for action."

Suzy smiled. "They think of everything. Of course, there's no time for a nap in the middle of a campaign. I feel like I could walk for miles."

"Well, that won't be necessary. As soon as our soldiers have eaten and cleaned up their camp, we'll be on our way. The caravan will continue and you get to ride."

"You know, I think I'll walk with the soldiers. I need the exercise and I need to know what it's like to walk in their shoes as well." Her eyes twinkled. "In fact, I'll begin right now by serving these dedicated soldiers; they provided us such a fantastic meal. One good turn deserves another."

Both laughed and moved into position to act as servers. The soldiers who sat down were both surprised and pleased. As other caravan members finished eating, they too rose and followed the example of the two women. Marlen watched and nodded his approval when Suzy's eyes met his.

-21-

During that afternoon and the next morning the company moved on. Suzy enjoyed this part of the journey; the soldiers showed her a good time. They were amazed with their princess – she served them at mealtime, she walked along side them as they marched through the countryside, participated in their activities and talked to them when they had time. Everyone became more familiar and relaxed. This was done without affecting their surveillance; preparedness for combat and defence wasn't diminished by the more friendly tone of the trip.

Suzy saw some of the places she had earlier visited. Vibrant growth replaced the former dreariness of the landscape. They passed by many destroyed structures and Marlen pointed out one pile of rubble, in particular. It had been the castle that housed the prison where Marlen was held captive and they met Blog, a wounded and desperate prisoner. From one of its towers Suzy had unleashed the light of the crystals that broke down the curtains of darkness and led to the freedom of the region. Now that fortress that had hidden deeds of dark horror lay exposed as a heap of useless rumble.

Farther on the company passed the site of the dark commander's defeat and the entrance to the rock cleft, which was the beginning of a secret way into the castle. That tunnel with walls that depicted events that took place in Gorn led right into the lower reaches of the castle and prison. Here the soldiers had built a monument commemorating the deed; a small group of soldiers stood guard and provided tours and talks about the mighty deeds of the princess and the prince. Suzy felt a wave of embarrassment that the simple act of helping to free the land was being memorialized. Marlen and Sapphira were quick to explain how grateful these people were to be free and in the light. The journey beyond the cave was uneventful although the close proximity to the dark forces increased the level of alertness from moderate to extreme.

The following afternoon the company of soldiers and the caravan reached a spot where the lush green plains dotted with trees abruptly ended. A vast tract of brackish sand on which nothing grew lay before them, an empty, lifeless wasteland, in stark contrast to the region through which they had just passed.

The deathly stillness of the stagnant desert produced a foreboding of tragedy and destruction. The happy and almost boisterous conversations of a day ago were now hushed whispers or simple silence as all gazed out at this dismal setting. They joined a much larger force of men who were already in position. Blog had command of these men.

Suzy looked for her friend but remained discreetly in the background so as not to interfere with the operation of the troop. She knew that his responsibilities as commander would consume much of his time. Meanwhile, she was content – she would make contact with him later.

Suzy wondered what the next step was going to be. Surely, the dark commander knew this force had arrived on his doorstep. Now the waiting game began. Suzy didn't know or understand military strategy and tactics; what she did know was that evil was always the enemy and every effort towards its elimination must be made whenever it reared its ugly head.

Suzy knew that the commanders and the Sages were often meeting to determine the proper course of action. She would be informed at the proper time.

Suzy gazed over the desolation that stretched away from her. Somewhere out there was a dark area wherein resided forces determined to wreak havoc and bring absolute chaos to all of Gorn. *We must stop that force. The future growth and prosperity of this great land depends on the success of all of us - Sages, Blog, his soldiers, me. We must lead the people into a brighter tomorrow. Am I prepared to help? You bet I am.*

Suddenly, she felt a heavy weight pulling down on her neck. She raised her hand to grasp the necklace, which seemed to weigh more than usual. She lifted it with her hand; now, it didn't seem to weigh more than it did before. *Strange, I thought it felt heavy.*

She released the gems so they again rested against her skin. The necklace no longer seemed heavy but one of the gems felt warmer than the rest. She gingerly moved the three jewels, determining that the heat was coming from the spherical one. When she lifted it in her fingers, she couldn't notice any difference in its temperature from the others. She felt all of the gems - there definitely wasn't any difference. *Hmmm, this is baffling.*

She returned the necklace to its usual position. She now could feel a slight vibrating motion against the nape of her neck. *One of the jewels is moving.* Again, after careful observation she determined that the spherical crystal was behaving differently. *That does it, I must see Marlen about this. I'm sure he'll have an idea about what's going on.*

She stood up and made her way towards the command tent. The soldiers didn't make any effort to stop her movements although she could tell she was under their constant surveillance.

Before she reached the command tent, Marlen emerged from the enclosure and smiled at her. “Suzy, you’rc just on time. We need to talk about the strategy that’ll be used over the next few days.”

This is more than coincidental. Suzy frowned. “Marlen, I was on my way to talk to you. Something strange has just happened.”

Marlen held up his hand indicating that Suzy should wait. She nodded and followed as he entered another tent. Upon entering, she realized it was Marlen’s. No one else was in it. He sat down in a chair and pointed to a bench nearby.

“We need to be very discreet. We’re very close to the enemy and we’ve captured another spy.”

Suzy interrupted her friend. “Here! That’s a surprise! I thought all the soldiers were loyal and dedicated.”

“Suzy, I’m sorry to be abrupt with you but I must talk with you and time’s short. The spy was part of the caravan - you need to know about his presence and the need for absolute vigilance. Don’t ever underestimate the power of the enemy who comes with promises that are so smooth and convincing. Before you know it, you’re drawn into his web without realizing the dangers. Enough of that! You know about the enemy and his tricks. Before we continue you said you had a question about something strange.”

“Marlen, the crystals are acting in a peculiar fashion - well, one in particular.” Suzy went on to tell Marlen about what she had just experienced with the spherical gem. Marlen listened carefully and then just sat in deep thought without asking to see the jewel in question. Suzy knew from previous conversations that he wouldn't touch the crystals so this didn't surprise her. She knew it wasn't a lack of interest. He rubbed his fingers and thumb over his face towards his mouth and then touched his temple with his fingers. He then cupped his chin and rested his face in his hand for a short time.

Suzy watched her friend. *I think this must be serious. Usually, he knows the answer without waiting.*

Marlen stood up, pacing back and forth briefly before turning to talk to Suzy. "That's an interesting development, dear princess. I believe we're getting a message from the crystals. Powerful magic resides within these unusual gems. The origin of the crystals is so ancient that we know very little about them. They appear to have been left by the Creator as a means to communicate with his people and as an aid for them in times of trouble. The Sages were taught that the crystals had disappeared from Gorn in the deep past so we were surprised when you found them lying in a meadow outside of Gorn. Obviously, they were meant for you to find. They may even have been there for a long time but only you were able to see them and pick them up. We know they were meant for only you because you're the one who senses their expressions and are able to unleash their enormous powers."

Suzy remained seated on the bench listening to the amazing history of the necklace. Her hand came to rest on the necklace. "Marlen, you mentioned a Creator who left them behind. Could you tell me more about him?"

Marlen smiled briefly. "We have deliberately not spoken about the Creator because, quite frankly, you know more about Him than most in Gorn. We didn't want to confuse you in what you've already learned."

Suzy was delighted with his response. She wanted to know more. "You said He left behind objects of power. What else did He leave?"

"As I said earlier we thought most were gone. At first, after He exiled people from his presence, he left the crystals of power to help them in their struggle. However, people forgot the reason for the crystals and began to use them for selfish motives. It was then the Sages were sent into the world to provide wisdom and guidance. Sages, at first, intermingled with the children of creation, marrying them with whom love did grow and nurturing new youth in the expanding family. Since the Sages are immortal, they lived to see their offspring grow, mature, age and, in some cases, be killed by accident or war. After many cycles had taken place most withdrew from the marriage experience and sought companionship within their dwindling group. Although we are immortal, we can be killed like any living being. Now, we remain to carry on the appointed tasks for all the people of Gorn until redemption comes to them as it has to your people. Enough of the past. Right now we must determine our course of action to upset the plans of the enemy." Marlen stopped pacing and returned to his chair where he seated himself.

"Suzy, out there's a darkness within which beats a malevolent heart dedicated to the ruin of all that's bright. We believe you're here because you can help us in our struggle. In the past, you arrived to be of assistance and now again we believe that's why you're here. Our troops are amassing a large force; we plan to issue Natas a challenge. While his attention's diverted, we'll enter the heart of his darkness to discover its source and to lift the veil. Since you were successful once before in accomplishing this task we hope you will once again play a key role. However, before we can proceed, I must give you the choice of whether you wish to participate. I am required by ancient protocol to do this. You are forewarned - there is danger involved since we'll be near to Natas, not a highly sought after place to be. Please consider the risks associated with this request before you give your answer."

Suzy sat through Marlen's explanation attentively giving it deep thought. She had been very interested in the early history of the Sages and their role in the life of Gorn. She knew that Marlen only sketched out the present crisis instead of describing it in detail. Marlen was concerned about her security and, of course, the risks were high - she knew that as well.

"Thank you, dear friend, for telling me the truth about what's about to happen and giving me the opportunity to go with into action. I'm dedicated to truth and the war on darkness, wherever it's fought. We're all called to be bearers of the light. I'm not sure what my role's going to be but the crystals seem to be saying that I'm to go ahead: my heart's also sending the same message. I'm ready, my friend."

Marlen nodded gravely, beckoning Suzy to follow as he rose from his chair and walked out of the tent. Sapphira, the other Sages and the commanders, including Blog were standing outside the command tent. The commanders came to attention and saluted both Marlen and Suzy.

Marlen simply said, "We move in the morning. Let's rest up and get prepared."

Everyone knew what Suzy had decided without being told. They were pleased to be making a move against the dark one.

-22-

Timmy stood at the top of the hill they had just climbed and looked down on a tranquil valley in which stood a tall citadel-like tower with the banner of the Sages fluttering in the light breeze. Tasha and Emeralda stood off to his left looking down into the valley. Their journey to these hills had been uneventful and unhindered. They spent two nights under the stars but nothing dangerous had shown up. Water had been plentiful and they had found sufficient food to supplement the rations packed along with them.

Overall, Timmy admired his old foe for preparing so well for this trip. He took in the beautiful scene below him. My old foe has some deep dark secrets that plague her, haunting her nights and pursuing her thoughts everyday. Emeralda really believes this dark lord, Natas, is following her, driving her on with a reckless abandon. However, there's more, which she manages to hide most of the time. She isn't able to cover it up during the night when dark nightmares visit her to keep her from having a good rest. What phantoms haunt her quiet moments?

Both nights as they crossed the plains Emeralda had suffered dreams of horror but she refused to admit that anything was happening. Somehow, the closer they came to this location the more intense the trauma appeared to grip her. Timmy was certain that the origin lay in the past through her prolonged exposure to the lodestone. Her subsequent denial of its effects and continued refusal to seek help to overcome the madness meant that she could not escape from suffering the nightly pain.

Timmy looked up at the sun. There was enough daylight to journey into the valley but not enough to explore the castle this evening. He studied the locale from this point to gain some knowledge of the trip ahead. He was at a disadvantage since his adversary knew this location like the back of her hand. *Well, no use prolonging the agony.*

He turned to his companions. "By the position of the sun we should be able to get into the valley and set up camp before dark."

Emeralda liked the suggestion. She had been standing in utter indecision. She desired to transform and soar on wings into the valley to expedite the travel and to reach her most sought after goal as quickly as possible but she couldn't enter the valley in a transformed condition. She could feel the adrenaline flowing through her body and the excitement of achieving her goal. She was near elation at the thought of reaching out for…. She abruptly stopped thinking about her goal as she glanced over at her companions. They hadn't given any indication of knowing her thoughts but maybe they were letting her fall into a trap. Cold fear washed over her; she dreaded being this close to her baby and the cause of her pain and anguish. She was mortified at the opportunity to actually be in its presence again but likewise fascinated by the chance to have her baby back. She had stood there pondering what to do when Timmy announced the decision for her. *What a relief!*

Tasha surveyed the beautiful setting noting that the castle was built within a bend of a flowing brook so that the approach to its main entrance could only be made from the west. Fortunately, they were on the same side of the brook as the castle so they did not have to be concerned with crossing the stream. Off to the south at a considerable distance she detected a bridge with a small tower at one end. The space surrounding the castle appeared to be rolling hills without trees growing in the immediate proximity of the walls. She also noted a small stone structure, like a shed, set off to the northwest of the castle - about fifty paces from a bend in the brook. What Tasha really noticed was the quiet serenity without any apparent movement of creatures. *Best be observant and careful.* She really had not thought one way or the other knowing that the castle was their destination and the arrival there was merely a matter of timing.

After following Emeralda down a winding path lined with blossoming shrubs, the fragrance of which was heavy and rich like that of lilac, the party made its way over several small hills to a larger hill on which they found a low stone bench. Here they had rested a few, drinking some water. Shadows were lengthening; in an hour or so, the valley would be completely in shade. They looked out at the castle, which now stood brightly in the sunlight.

Timmy turned to the others. "I suggest we make our way to that stone shed where we can set up camp for the night."

Emeralda pointed towards the castle. "Young prince, wouldn't we be wise to go straight to the castle. We must be quick so as to avoid detection…." Emeralda paused too long before continuing. "…By Natas who's sure to have watchers in place."

Tasha and Timmy exchanged glances, knowing their foe was still as deceitful and dangerous as ever. Timmy decided he had to reply firmly and clearly.

"If Natas knows this location we would never have made it this far. Let's not be overly anxious. Tasha and I don't know the lay of the land or the floor plan of the castle. I know you do; before we can walk into that building, we need you to tell us all about it. While we have the evening meal you can brief us on what's inside. Tomorrow, after a long and restful night, we can go onto the castle. I'm sure the stone will be safe that long."

Tasha smiled as Emeralda frowned. Both Timmy and Tasha knew she was disappointed but neither were surprised with her comment. "I suppose you're right again. I'm coming to see that it has to be your way, not that I'm complaining. I'm more than happy that you're here and, of course, I'm more than willing to share with you what I know of this place. Yes, setting up camp by that shed's a good idea. We can always use it as a shelter should we need to get out of poor weather or are attacked by marauders."

They made their way across the plain to the shed where they set up camp. Timmy went down to the water's edge where he gathered dry driftwood from along the shore, deposited there during flood times. This he carried to where his partners were unpacking the supplies. He prepared a fireplace by scratching away the grass cover and placing small stones in a circle. He then gathered small clumps of dry grass and small twigs. Over this collection, he stacked the larger branches and then some logs to form a tripod. From his pack he withdrew his flint and metal.

He looked around to make sure the others weren't watching. He removed the bracelet from the pouch, stooped over his fireplace and placed a small twig inside the bracelet. Immediately, it began to smolder and glow. He held it inside the nest of grass he had gathered. A couple of deep breaths into the mass caused it to ignite into a small flame. He added more kindling as the fire became hotter. Soon he knew he could leave it to grow on its own. He carefully replaced the bracelet in the pouch and the flint and metal in the pack.

Tasha and Emeralda remained preoccupied with meal preparation. Timmy returned to the stream to gather more driftwood and as he stood by its shore, he observed trout leaping from the water. He removed his footwear, rolled up his pant legs and made his way into the brook. The cold water swirled around his legs and felt very refreshing on muscles made sore by the long journey. He stooped over, standing quietly with his hands apart in the water. As he stood there, he realized that the water was very cold; it began to send icy needles through him. He could only be there for a short time before the frigid knives drove him out. Timmy spotted movement and he reacted with lightning speed grabbing a trout and in one motion, tossing it to the shore. He moved his legs to warm up, bent over and caught another fish. He remained in the water for three more attempts; after another success he quickly came out of the water. Timmy sat on the shore kicking his feet, flicking off the water and restoring warmth in his chilled legs and feet.

The valley was almost in complete shadow as he made his way to the campsite carrying his catch and a couple of logs. Tasha looked up as he pointed towards the castle. The shadow was creeping up the highest turret to where the flag shone in bright sunlight. The spike at the top of the flagstaff was gleaming as it reflected the last rays of the setting sun. The intensity of the reflected brilliance grew brighter and brighter until, for one brief moment, the tip sparkled like the evening star in all its glory; then it was gone leaving the valley in the gathering gloom. They stared for a few seconds; a low cackle broke the spell.

"Don't let the stars get in your eyes. Let's get a meal going."

Timmy and Tasha chuckled as they set to work cleaning the fish and preparing the meal.

Much later, the three sat around the fire preparing for their bedtime. Nothing was said as they stared into the glowing embers; each sensed an oppressing weight bearing down on them. Off in the distance stood the ominous shadow of the castle, which seemed to swim in closer when they didn't look in that direction. It was hard not to think about the castle. Timmy looked at Tasha. "Wasn't that a marvelous sight earlier this evening, like a rare diamond caught in a beam of sunlight."

Tasha smiled, "It was amazing, like a beacon signalling good news. I hope it is, since the presence of that darkened castle seems so foreboding."

"I know what you mean. It seems as though that castle's trying to scare us away. I don't understand it; I just know that I'm not comfortable here."

Emeralda listened to the young people talking. When she heard about the sparkling point, she laughed to herself. These young people are so naive as to think it was a signal. They have no idea the influence the lodestone can have over anyone in its vicinity – I should warn them since I need Timmy to be clearheaded at the right time.

"The lodestone's a powerful weapon for warding off the dark forces. It can move and turn lesser minds, even powerful ones. Around it is a force field that's kept in place to protect the stone - it too can affect minds at a distance so that they loathe approaching it. What you're feeling may in fact be that sensation. In order to do any work around it you must master that repulsion."

"Emeralda, what are you sensing now from the stone?" Timmy asked. "You've often referred to it as your child. What's your child saying to you now that you're so close?"

Emeralda's eyes opened and fixed Timmy in a deliberate and chilly stare. What do you mean by that, silly prince. I wish you wouldn't intrude into my private affairs.

She sighed. Take your time; get a grip on yourself; let it go. These two certainly have away of getting my goat. I get so stirred up that I say things without thinking.

"Actually, I've felt nothing nor heard any voices. I'm somewhat surprised by that since, in the past, my baby's called out to me whenever I was nearby. I sense the field is still in place but, of course, we need to actually enter the stone room to be completely certain."

Timmy wasn't sure what to make of that reply. Emeralda didn't deny having heard the stone calling out in the past and didn't seem to be lying in her reply. *Remain skeptical about anything Emeralda says; the look on Tasha's face confirms the way I feel.*

Tasha spoke up first. "We should turn in now and have a good night's sleep. We need all the rest we can get because tomorrow's going to be a busy day."

Emeralda was happy to have the conversation diverted. Soon, everyone had turned in; silence slipped over the camp as the logs burned lower and lower.

Emeralda looked around; surprised to see that the entire valley had completely filled with fog obscuring everything from sight. A deep dread prodded her thoughts as she tried to determine which direction the castle lay. She took a few steps and suddenly the ground gave way - she was falling. The mist flew by her. She caught glimpses of shadowy hands reaching through the foggy shroud to grab her. Once or twice, she felt them make contact with her outstretched hands but they failed to grab her. Emeralda felt sharp nails raking her arms as they failed to grapple on to her hands. Groaning came from deep in the mist but she couldn't see its source. She could just make out a low sobbing, which cried out to her. She didn't hear it with her ears but could feel the sobbing deep within her chest. Within her head, she could feel a sharp pain like hot needles driven into her skull. Emeralda wanted this senseless descent to stop but refused to reach for or grab anything - somehow she knew it wouldn't do any good. The agony of waiting for the fall to end combined with the pain she was feeling in her head caused her to begin a low undulating moan. She wanted to stop, to control it but couldn't gain any mastery over her reaction.

Suddenly, Emeralda was very cold and shaking uncontrollably. She opened her eyes to find she was lying near the glowing logs. Her covers were pushed to her feet - she was cold; the night had cooled off so much. She glanced around the camp expecting to find Timmy watching her while leaning on one elbow. He, however, was curled up in his blanket with his face hidden in shadow. He appeared to be asleep. Tasha was tucked away in her covers facing the opposite direction. The moon was waning to the last quarter; its light, though not intense, still permitted one to make out the castle in the distance.

Emeralda again looked at her companions, feeling certain that they were sound asleep, stood up and stretched. She then made her way to the little stone shed and pushed open the door. She allowed herself enough time to scan the camp before she entered the shed through the open door, which she closed behind her.

-23-

From the shadow of his covers, Timmy watched Emeralda endure another nightmare. Her suffering manifested itself through violent thrashing about, kicking her covers to the end of her sleeping area, squeezing her head with both hands, uncontrolled panting and the emitting of an almost guttural wail. Unlike the previous episodes, Timmy waited before he intervened. He wanted to see whether Emeralda would behave differently. *It's obvious to me that she's in the grip of some unknown horror that continues to return and haunt her whenever she goes to sleep.* He controlled the urge to race over and place a healing hand on her. He remembered all too vividly the last time he touched her.

He watched her get up furtively and sneak carefully away from the campsite. *What's she up to now?* He prepared to jump up quickly should she come back, putting them under attack. He watched her stop by the stone shed and peer around checking out the surroundings. Timmy remained under his blankets so as not to reveal his observations. He continued to breathe in a relaxed manner to maintain his readiness. As she entered the shed, he rose quietly so as not to disturb the fast asleep Tasha. He cautiously lifted his weapons belt and held it firmly in his hand as he picked up his boots. With these items in hand, he made his way towards the shed. At the entrance to the shed, Timmy stopped, slipped on his boots and fastened his belt in place. He looked about the campsite and briefly considered waking Tasha. When he saw everything was in order and the evening was quiet he dismissed that thought. *I'll be able to slip away more effectively by myself – besides, Emeralda has to be followed as quickly as possible.* He listened at the doorway but couldn't hear any sounds from within. He opened the door quietly and entered the darkened shed.

As his eyes adjusted to the gloom, Timmy could make out the outline of a closed door. He pushed and felt it yield. Beyond he saw a set of stairs descending into the ground. As he stepped on to the second step, the rest of the stairway lit up, light coming from some small round stones placed along the line where the floor joined the walls. He made his way to the bottom of the stairs to find another doorway. As he pushed this door open, the light in the stairwell went out but the hallway that stretched away lit up. He listened but only silence met his ears. Timmy realized that Emeralda must be moving quickly through the passageway because she was familiar with this route. *Crafty witch, this was one of those secrets she kept from us. Probably because we didn't directly ask her about it.* He grinned since he had come to realize exactly how she reasoned.

Timmy looked around and saw that the tunnel was well-made; its walls and roof were arched with well-shaped and fitted stones. Some of the stones were sculpted, carved to represent scenes from the forest and the plains. This passageway obviously was made for traffic to and from wherever it was going because it was spacious. Timmy had no doubt that its purpose when it was built was as a secret way to the castle. He also noticed as he moved along the corridor the lights ahead continued to come on while those that he had passed would darken.

After walking along the passageway for a short time while admiring the handiwork, Timmy came to a closed door. He saw a ring hanging from the side of the door opposite the large black hinges. He pulled on the ring and the door swung towards him. He stepped aside as the door moved past and he walked over the threshold to find he was at the foot of another set of stairs. To his right Timmy saw a second door. As he stepped into the stairwell the lights of the passageway went out and the door swung closed quietly. The stairwell was gloomy so he moved to the second door and pushed it open. A newly-lit tunnel stretched away before him – its appearance was much like the previous one. Timmy stepped back and allowed the door to close. He stepped on to the first step and then on to the second. *Just as I expected, the stairway lights have come on.* He was certain that Emeralda would have come by this way so he climbed the stairs to the door at the top. He listened a moment, then grabbed the ring and pulled the door open. Timmy stepped into a much darker room, lit only by meagre moonlight entering through narrow windows. He was in the castle.

Timmy moved silently across the room to the hallway that led off to the left. He waited a moment to listen and then set off down the hallway. He felt a pleasant sensation washing over him as he walked. He passed several doors and corridors without stopping, which seemed to be the right thing to do. The sensation grew as he moved. He felt better and better. Ahead he could hear an indistinct groaning. Timmy rounded a corner and saw a doorway to a room. *That room's better lit than this corridor.*

He cautiously walked towards the entry. He noticed the light was coming from the top of a pedestal on which sat a large very ornate and beautiful stone. Kneeling on the floor, he saw Emeralda with both arms reaching out to the stone. Her eyes appeared closed.

Suddenly she began to speak in a low wail. "My beautiful child, you know I'm always here to help you, wanting to be next to you, to hold you in my arms and close to my heart. I can feel your wonderful presence; you call me here. It's so beautiful to know that you wanted me, that you called for me. Now you hiss at me, you send out needles to sting me. Why, little one, do you treat me so badly? Don't you remember your dear Emeralda. I stayed with you for many years, enjoying your calling and your company. You have to remember dear Emeralda, my sweet thing. I was there with you for so long. It's not my fault that you've been left on your own for all this time. I'd never have done that to you if I had you in my safe keeping. Oh! How I want you in my arms even though I remember how badly you bit me. Why'd you do that to me, your dear mother? Oh! I can't reach any farther because you keep pushing me away."

Emeralda began to grunt and groan as she tried to move closer to the stone but the force field repelled her efforts. Timmy stood still, almost mesmerized at the sight of his mighty foe powerless against the force field. He felt a deep sense of sympathy for her; Emeralda had little, if any, control over the desires driving her. He considered intervening but suddenly felt a tug at his neck. The pouch seemed much heavier. *I'm needed elsewhere, back at the campsite*. Timmy considered for a brief moment staying with Emeralda. *I'd better hurry back to Tasha. Emeralda's not going anywhere, she'll be okay on her own.*

Timmy set off at a run retracing his journey through the castle, down the staircase, through the tunnels and up the far stairs. He continued to feel the weight of the bracelet around his neck. He pulled open the door of the shed quietly and stood within the darkened interior looking out over the camp.

He could make out two figures standing within the campsite. One was leaning over Tasha who was struggling to free herself from her covers and the grip of her captor. The other was standing back watching the struggle.

Timmy couldn't see who the assailants were in the darkness. He had to act immediately. He clutched the pouch, slid his hand into the band and drew his short sword. Timmy noticed that his sight was heightened and the scene before him was very clear. He knew he was no longer visible but his sword was glowing a bright green.

As Timmy stepped from the shed, he raised his sword and shouted. "Stop! Let her go!" He began to run across the space separating him from the attackers.

The two intruders straightened up at the sound of his voice. The one leaning over Tasha gasped, dropping the rope he held; the other threw his hands in the air. The very blood in their veins curdled at the horrifying sight bearing down on them; they froze in their tracks. A green sword waving through the semi-darkness approached as they stood riveted in their tracks. What type of apparition was about to seize them?

Suddenly, each screamed in horror and the fright instinct took over. The one supervising the attack began to flee down the path away from the castle. His partner hesitated only a brief moment before following his commander in a hot retreat from the plain. They didn't look back as they fled in horror and fear for their lives.

Tasha struggled with her covers - she too was horrified by the spectacle of the approaching, wildly swinging sword.

Timmy watched the fleeing enemy and turned towards Tasha who stared, terrified by his raised sword. He quickly realized that she couldn't see him since he was wearing his bracelet. He removed it and as he returned it to its pouch, he spoke softly to Tasha. "Tasha, it's me. Don't panic. I know you've just had a terrible experience but those attackers are gone. It's me, Timmy, Tasha, easy does it now. I'm back and the attackers have fled. You're looking at the sword that Emeralda gave to me. I don't know why it glowed but it sure worked in scaring off that terrible pair. I'm here now so take it easy; breathe slowly."

Tasha threw aside her covers and looked about frantically. She stared at Timmy as he stepped into the campsite and into the light. She brought up her sword, which she had finally withdrawn from its scabbard that had been entangled with her covers. Timmy ignored the sword and reached for some small pieces of wood, which he placed on the fire. As the blaze began to grow and cast more light around the camp, Tasha was able to clearly see that it was Timmy. She slowly lowered her weapon.

"Where have you been? Where's Emeralda? Did she send that pair of thugs into the camp? Why would you leave me to the designs of a pair like that? I was terrified about what they wanted. They stood there leering down at me. They seemed to enjoy the terror they instilled in me. What's going on here?"

Timmy replaced his sword in his scabbard and turned to face Tasha. He had left assuming all was fine in the valley. This attack came as a total surprise to him since he was sure that Emeralda would have warned them of an impending danger. He saw Tasha was starting to shake as the shock of the evening was finally settling in.

"I'm back, Tasha. I won't leave you again. Here, wrap yourself in these blankets. Then you sit near the fire. You need to warm up and feel the comfort of the blankets. I'll explain what I know but I'm as baffled as you are with what happened here. I'll tell as much as I know. Here, let me help you move."

Timmy stepped over to where Tasha was trying to pick up her blankets while still holding on to her sword. She was shaking too hard to grasp the covers firmly. He scooped them up. He placed his other hand on her shoulder and directed her towards a sitting log near the fire.

As soon as he made contact with her, Timmy sensed her relaxing; she allowed him to guide her towards the seat. Tasha moved slowly unsure of her step but determined to do things on her own. She appreciated his gentle touch and direction. She also felt her anxiety quickly dispersing and her sense of confidence and security rapidly returning. Tasha sat down, allowing Timmy to drape the blankets over her and tuck them in around her.

Timmy sat down opposite her so that he could look directly into her face. He began to tell what had happened that evening. He filled her in on Emeralda's actions. *Tasha needs to know everything; Emeralda's the central figure to us getting out of here.* He considered withholding information about his bracelet but then the story would be incomplete; there would be no explanation for the green sword without a swordsman.

He took some time to tell the story of the bracelet, its acquisition and its effects on others. Tasha had sat through the entire explanation, astonished at the fantastic story she was being told. Part of her wanted to deny what she was hearing as rubbish or myth but she knew what she had seen and experienced; she didn't have a better explanation for it. She stared as Timmy gently took the bracelet from the pouch around his neck and showed it to her. *I'd better warn her about the bracelet.*

"I told you what happened when Suzy tried to put it on. She suffered a terrible burn to her hand; we were warned that it'll likely happen to anyone else who tries. In fact, I tried to pass a leather strap through it to hold it in place around my neck and the leather sizzled and burned. In a moment, I'm going to put it on. I'll vanish from your sight but will still be here. You can reach out and touch me. I can still hold things. Some disappear with me while others don't, like the sword that Emeralda gave to me."

Tasha shrugged in her blanket as she re-adjusted it on her shoulders. "Why does the sword glow with a bright green colour when you wave it? It certainly catches your eye."

"That I don't know. Maybe it has something to do with the bracelet. I don't know. We'll try a few tests after I show you the effect of the bracelet."

Timmy slid his hand into the band. Tasha let out a short gasp of surprise despite being forewarned what would happen. She shrank from where Timmy had been sitting, then she smiled, reached across and felt his hand where it had been previously. She felt him removing the bracelet and suddenly she could see him sitting as he had before. He placed the band in the pouch and secured it around his neck under his shirt, out of sight.

"Needless to say, the bracelet and its effects must always be kept secret. Emeralda doesn't know about it nor do many others"

"Gosh! I feel privileged that you'd tell me about your secret. We only met a short time ago and already you trust me enough to know about the bracelet. I intend to keep our secret."

"We're in this adventure together, Tasha. I can't expect you to trust me if I keep things hidden from you."

"I won't let you down. You've done so much; I appreciate the fact that you wouldn't withhold a secret like this from me."

Timmy held up a finger for silence and slowly removed his sword from its scabbard. A bright green glow shone from it at once. He slid the sword back into its sheath and then he looked at Tasha.

"You draw it from the scabbard. Let's see what it does for you."

Tasha smiled in appreciation and pulled the sword partially from its resting place. It began to glow a bright green as it had before. She then pulled it completely free and suddenly it felt so heavy that the tip dropped to the ground; she could barely hold on to the handle.

She grimaced at the effort of holding it. "I can barely lift this sword. What's happening here? Mine's very light but I can't hold on to your sword much longer."

Timmy reached over and closed his hand gently over Tasha's. He easily lifted both her hand and the sword. He raised it into position and slid it back into its scabbard. Then he released the handle and her hand.

Tasha drew back and examined her hand. "That was very unusual. Either the sword became heavy or my arm and hand lost all their strength. I've never experienced anything like that before."

Timmy shook his head. "Many things in Gorn are very different and unusual. You begin to expect it after a while. Now I'm curious about your sword. You said it's very light in your hand. I'm going to draw it from your scabbard." He looked over to where she had set it down, "Oh, you didn't replace it in its scabbard."

"No, I suppose I didn't. Those attackers really shook me up - then some ghost sword came flying through the air. You wouldn't expect me to remember a simple thing like putting my sword away after all of that."

"No, I guess I shouldn't." Both laughed.

He reached down to pick up the sword; the weight of it surprised him. He dropped to one knee to give himself more leverage. He placed both hands on the handle and was able to raise it very slowly.

"Yeah, right!" Tasha watched Timmy brace himself. "Now you mock me with your act."

"That may be what it looks like, Tasha, but let me assure you this is no act. Your blade's very heavy and cumbersome to hold. Here! Take it in your hands."

Tasha stood up, dropping her blankets to the ground. She no longer shook from the cold or shock. She was amazed at the difficulty Timmy seemed to have. As she closed her right hand over the handle and brushed by his hands, she could feel the tension in his fingers. She grasped the handle firmly and took control of the weapon as Timmy loosened his grip on the handle. The sword felt light and free in her hand as she swept it safely away from Timmy and moved it in a circle before her. It was fantastic how good it felt in her hand. Tasha moved over, picked up the scabbard, and deposited the sabre into its place.

Timmy was grinning as she looked up. Her face shone with confidence and astonishment. She put her right hand to her mouth and raised the scabbard over her head with her left. "Wow!"

Tasha lowered the scabbard and turned to Timmy. "What does this mean? Why's my sword so light but yours is so heavy?"

Timmy shook his head. "I don't know why. No one's ever explained anything like this to me before but I can only guess. Since we received these weapons from Emeralda, some special power of the Sages must reside within them. The bearer is meant to have a particular sword, not a different one. We can easily handle our own but we find the others difficult to wield. Mine has the extra property of a glow that doesn't depend on who draws it. It has a purpose."

"Like scaring the daylights out of everyone. Did you see how those two scoundrels fled?"

"Not to mention its effect on you."

They both laughed and then Timmy looked up. "Speaking of daylight." He pointed to the eastern sky over the valley. The sky was becoming lighter as night was making its retreat.

Tasha yawned. "I think I'll try to get a little more sleep. I don't think we're in any danger from attack since a ghost sword seems to protect this valley."

Timmy laughed with her. "I believe you're right. A little sleep would be better than none at all. Emeralda's not going anywhere. I don't think she'll bother us any more tonight. Let's sleep for a few hours; in the morning we can explore the castle and check on her."

Each gathered their belongings and wandered back to the campfire and the places they had set out for themselves. Timmy added a couple of larger logs to maintain the fire. They curled up in their covers and fell asleep before the flames had really caught, setting the wood ablaze.

-24-

Before sunrise, Suzy woke up, dressed and prepared for the events of the day ahead of her. After a wash, she made certain her crystals were in place, lying coolly against her neck. She also wore the little golden chain, to which was fastened the emerald stud that she had found. *Emeralda's sure looked for this. She keeps coming back to our yard but so far hasn't found it. Oh, look! There's some light chain armour, lying on the table. I wonder if Marlen left that.*

Suzy lifted the armour and slid it over her head so that it now covered her necklaces. She turned her attention to the small acorn shaped helmet that she tried on her head. Suzy wasn't surprised to see how well it fitted; her companions seemed to know everything about her. She fastened the chinstrap and adjusted it for the proper tension. Suzy then looked at the short scabbard before her. She lifted it, placed the belt around her waist, and fastened the buckle. It hung lightly on her left side. She unsnapped the strap holding the handle firmly in place and slowly drew the blade from its place of rest. As she did, the blade began to glow with an emerald hue. Suzy removed the short sword completely from the scabbard and held it before her face. It lay lightly in her hand, barely noticeable for weight. She swung it a couple of times and was pleased with its response. She returned it to its scabbard and secured it in place once again. *I hope it's unnecessary but I know how careful Sapphira and Marlen are. They're taking no chances with my safety.* That, in itself, relieved her of a great deal of anxiety that she might otherwise have felt.

She could hear the camp busily going about the business of preparing for a day that promised to be action packed. I wonder if I should stay in the tent until called or do I go out. I haven't any idea what I can do in getting ready. Oh well, in the past the soldiers always found something for me to do. I'll check with them.

Suzy hesitated by the door, closed her eyes and said a short benediction. Then she pushed open the flap of the tent and stepped into the camp.

Soldiers were moving everywhere, already fitted with their weapon and auxiliary support packs. She gazed about looking for her special friend knowing that Blog would likely be very busy elsewhere. It didn't stop her from scanning the camp. She was more than a little surprised to hear his voice just behind her.

"Princess, I wondered how long you'd sleep. It's good that you were able to because you'll need all your energy for today. Shortly, your party's going to leave while it's still fairly dark. The moon'll provide some light to make the going easier at first. Before you go, visit the cook camp to have a good breakfast and receive your ration pack. Eat well even if you don't feel up to it. You're going to need it. God bless you on your way."

Blog placed his right hand on her left shoulder and stood quietly for a moment. His blessing filled her with pleasure and assurance. He stepped back, saluted her and disappeared into the activity. She stood for a moment and chose that time for prayers of supplication and intercession.

She followed Blog's instructions by making her way to the cook camp. Several soldiers were eating their morning meal. When Suzy entered their midst, they saluted her and continued with their meal. She found a plate and a bowl and helped herself. She ate a bowl of thick porridge topped with honey and goat's milk. She returned to fill her plate with eggs and some sausages, which she arranged around four thin cakes over with some honey poured over them. *My goodness, they have a great cook. Everything on my plate looks delicious.*

When Suzy finished, she was tempted to get up and prepare to leave. She remembered Blog's instructions and went back for another sausage as well as a large piece of brown bread. Over this, she spooned a sticky mix of berries and grains. She picked up a cup of the clear soldiers' beverage. *This meal should hold me for the best part of the day. Rather than wolf this down in a hurry I'm going to take my time mixing each mouthful with a small sip of the drink.* When she was chewing the last few morsels, Sapphira joined her, bringing a sausage wrapped in a piece of brown bread.

Sapphira smiled. "It's good to see you prepared for our journey. Marlen and I ate our morning meal earlier and have been going over our plans again. I came to have a bit more to eat and to get you. We'll be leaving in a few minutes."

Suzy finished her food and looked over at her friend who had started eating. "The soldiers look like they're busy making their preparations."

"They've their preparations to make. They'll be making a big move after we're gone, From now on we don't discuss what they are or will be doing - we only talk about our activities when planning. We'll be holding a briefing session just before we set off. After that, it'll be important we know exactly what must be done without having to repeat the discussion. We're certain about the security of each member of our group, but we can never be absolutely sure. We've been finding too many spies within the camp."

Suzy nodded. Sapphira finished her food and rose to her feet. Suzy knew one thing: stick with Sapphira now and she'd find out soon enough what she needed to know. Two men, one in long, flowing, yellow-orange robes and the other in loose burgundy shirt and trousers joined them. Suzy knew they were powerful Sages whose wisdom and powers were needed for this dangerous mission. She followed as they walked quickly and efficiently through the bustling camp. The group made its way to Marlen's tent; Suzy recognized it from a distance. All four came to a stop outside the tent and waited.

A moment later Suzy heard her name. "Suzy, please come into the tent," She recognized Marlen's voice as she lifted the flap. The other three stood impassively as she went in.

Marlen's tent looked the same as it had before except that a backpack sat near the door. *Marlen's ready to go.*

Marlen stood in the centre of the tent; his expression was grim. "Suzy, I need to have a short talk with you. The advance party is set to leave under cover of darkness just before dawn. We don't have a great deal of time but it should be sufficient. I've already spelled out what a serious and dangerous mission this is. You agreed to come along but I must once again ask you if that's truly your wish. You aren't a resident of Gorn and shouldn't feel compelled in any way to help in our time of troubles. Should you decide not to accompany us no one will think any less…."

Suzy raised her right hand to stop Marlen. "You're a dear friend and I thank you for being so concerned about my well-being. You're right - I'm not a resident of Gorn but three times, I've been called here. I feel deep down that there's a purpose for my being in Gorn and as such what right have I to question that. Back home, I was in the process of pledging my life to a fight against darkness and evil anywhere. I won't back down because it may be dangerous, or even life threatening. I've received a promise and I trust in it. Besides, with good friends like Sapphira and you with me, I feel confident against any dark commander."

"Thank you, then we'll leave shortly. You may return to Sapphira; ask the other two Sages to come in. I need to consult with them."

Suzy nodded and backed out of the tent. She turned and faced the two Sages, "Marlen wishes the two of you to go in."

After they went into the tent Suzy looked towards her friend. Sapphira smiled at her. "I'm pleased that you're coming with us. Soon, we'll be talking about the first part of our action. Let's join the others and be informed about that part of the plan."

The briefing was very short; Marlen told them two soldiers would join the five of them and that they would be leaving in fifteen minutes. Sapphira and Suzy returned to their tents together and picked up their pre-packed sacks and weapons. They made their way back to Marlen's tent where he stood waiting for them with his pack firmly in place, his hood drawn over his head and his hand gripping his staff which seemed to support his entire weight. When all seven had gathered, they set off together following Marlen through the busy camp. No one in the camp seemed to pay any attention as the party moved through the bustling mass of humanity. They moved into the darkness beyond the camp and made their way along a low line of shrubs, which ended near a large tree that stood darkly silhouetted against the dimly lit sky. Marlen held up one hand to stop Suzy who was following a short distance behind him. The group paused and Suzy sensed Sapphira and the Sages move into place behind her. She didn't hear or see the soldiers who seemed to have disappeared.

The night was very still with only the occasional cricket singing a solitary tune. Suzy realized her sense of hearing was much more acute as she heard the almost silent breathing of her companions and the slithering sound of a snake disturbed by their presence. She almost jumped when she saw a soldier quietly slip in beside Marlen, so silently had he moved.

Suzy heard him whisper to the commander, "As we feared we didn't leave unnoticed. We caught a member of the caravan trailing us. We'd long suspected him but could never get enough to prove it. He won't be making any further reports to his commander and won't be a problem to anyone else. We'll remain vigilant because our enemy can be very devious."

The soldier slipped into the darkness and Marlen began his march into that darkness. Suzy and the rest of the party followed as the group made its way past the line of trees into the open desert. It was dark enough to conceal their movements but the barest of light from the stars and the setting moon allowed them to pick out a safe path over the rocky terrain. Marlen picked up the pace since it was imperative that they reach their goal or at least a place of shelter before daybreak. Suzy at first found the pace a bit difficult but she allowed her well-rested body to establish the routine and soon it was easy to keep up. She was exhilarated to march in unison with her troop.

After an undetermined period of time during which the quick march continued, Marlen led the group up a rocky ridge that cut across the direction in which they were going. The pace was slower during the climb. Choosing a safe and quiet way was accomplished with great care. Suzy felt some apprehension as they neared the top of the ridge since they were nearing the region of darkness; this height of land provided excellent ground for ambush. Marlen paused and the company came to a halt. Everyone waited for their commander's signal, using the time to catch their breath and stretch tired muscles. Suzy was amazed at how quickly she recovered and didn't even feel thirsty. Suddenly, a figure came out of the darkness from the top of the ridge. She identified him as the soldier who had earlier reported to Marlen.

In undertones he reported to Marlen. "The way over the ridge is clear. My companion and I did a quick but thorough scout of this place. We didn't come across any of the enemy, although there are some traces of a small group being here in the recent past. We can continue over this ridge and down a rough path ahead." He departed and Marlen set out again. Everyone picked fell into line as the troop crossed the ridge and began the downward trek.

Off in the east the sky was beginning to lighten. Before long it would be too bright to continue so hurrying was an absolute necessity. Straight ahead, as she glanced past Marlen she noticed an area which was completely void and which blocked out the horizon, the light fringe of dawn and any starlight. This was the target: the group was attempting to reach that void before daybreak overtook them. Their march now took on a greater urgency as their goal was just within reach. Marlen began to unfurl a light rope, which he handed back to Suzy. She grabbed it in her left hand and passed it back to Sapphira using her right hand. Once Sapphira was pulling on it she allowed it to easily slip through the fingers of her left hand. Its movement came to a stop for a few moments and then continued several times. When the rope stopped moving, she flipped a loop and tied a knot to secure the loop. She then passed her left hand through the loop and grabbed the rope.

The wall of darkness loomed up before the group just as the eastern sky was turning a pink tinge. Marlen kept the group moving without stopping for instructions. He vanished a split second before Suzy too was engulfed in darkness. She allowed the rope to guide her as Marlen continued carefully to choose the path by using his staff. The pace naturally slowed as his progress was based on feel rather than on sight. Suzy was surprised that this darkness was different from what she had experienced before. As her eyes adjusted, she found she was able to ascertain shapes - Marlen before her, Sapphira behind her, her hand grasping the rope, rocks, and depressions. She found herself comparing it more to a thick fog than the deep of the night. Her thoughts were interrupted by Marlen's stopping.

The group moved in closer to allow a low whispered conversation. Marlen spoke softly, "Our movement will be very slow from now on in this impossible darkness. I find myself almost hesitating at the touch of each stone or the change in the slope of the land."

Suzy was surprised by this and even more so as the rest of her companions agreed about the intensity of the darkness. She decided to tell Marlen how she could see. "Marlen. I don't understand this at all. This darkness is little more than a fog, a deep gloom, to me. I'm able to make out shapes and even see each of you right now. I just assumed that was the case for all of you. It's something I think you should know."

Suzy watched as Sapphira shifted from one leg to another and as Marlen stroked his beard with his free hand. The soldiers remained motionless, awaiting a command. The Sages nodded their heads. *Are they mindlinking? No, they wouldn't dare mindlink so close to Natas. They must just be trying to figure out what to do next.*

"Most interesting development, my dear," Marlen whispered. "You continue to surprise and fascinate us with your special abilities here in Gorn. We're indeed fortunate that you're part of this group. I think you should take over the lead when we begin to move. Sapphira, Burgan, Gelder, do you continue to feel a presence? I have and it seems to be growing in strength."

The Sage in the burgundy shirt and loose fitting trousers spoke first. "The sensation grows stronger and more repulsive as we move deeper into this darkness."

Gelder, the other Sage, said, "We must be on the right track. Whatever's producing this vile feeling is much closer."

Sapphira joined the conversation. "We need to move on at once. Day has come and the troops are all in position and most vulnerable; they will be pressing beyond the boundaries and stirring up the wrath of Natas. The quicker we reach our goal the fewer casualties will occur."

This reminded Suzy that other things were also happening. Her good friend, Blog, would be leading those men and would be in a very dangerous position. *We must be on our way and can't be poky.*

Marlen spoke again. "We must press on to our goal. The troops are meant as a diversion, not as the vanguard of an invading force so let's get this mission done. Suzy, you'll exchange places with me taking the lead. I'll give you directions but you'll pick out the path since you can see. Take the lead ring of our line. I'll take yours but give me a moment to adjust it for my height. Take this time, any of you, to refresh yourselves."

Suzy stepped forward and as she did, she saw the soldiers come to attention and salute her. None of the party made any move to have a drink, a bite to eat nor seek relief. Suzy understood since she felt the same way. The wholesome breakfast with that refreshing drink continued to nourish and sustain all of them. She led the group off to find the source of the darkness.

Suzy found it easy going since she could see the lay of the land several paces ahead of her. She led the rest over the ground without hesitation so the pace of their walking increased. Occasionally, she felt Marlen's hand on her shoulder directing her to the right or to the left. As she continued, such signals diminished in number. Suzy was left to lead them freely on a path of her choosing. Every now and then, she felt icy fear grip her heart and sensed an oozy, slimy bubble in her mind. She strove hard to dismiss such thoughts and frequently dropped into silent prayer to overcome those moments.

Suzy recalled some of the lessons that Timmy and she had taken with Pastor Adams. These gave her strength to combat the sense of dread that grew as she continued on her way. Suzy felt assured by the promises given in those lessons; they were meant for her.

Something was near - something deeply horrid. She could feel herself sinking ever so slowly in something very sticky. As she went down, Suzy imagined something was pulling on her feet slowly. As she was sucked down, she felt something else pushing down on her shoulders to hasten her descent, a slow sinking into warm and slimy ooze.

Suzy plodded on closing her mind to the ever-increasing terror that kept rising within her. Her steps were shorter; her breathing more rapid. She wiped her hand across her eyes to clear her vision. Then she felt comfort as Marlen's hand gripped her shoulder.

"Let's stop here for a moment, my dear." Marlen's words were raspy and slurred; his breath was rapid. "How are you doing?"

Suzy expected him to continue but nothing more was forthcoming. She could see the Sages were bowed over as though under a great weight. The soldiers weren't standing at attention but were slouched over. The hidden horror was having a tremendous effect on all the members of the group.

"Marlen, I feel simply horrible. I'm trapped in an ooze that's pulling me under. It isn't real, I know that. I won't let it get the best of me." Suzy pulled herself up straight, stretching knotted muscles.

Marlin chuckled gravely. "This is why you're here. You show such resiliency by always bouncing back. Everyone - have a drink of refreshment and a small snack of that trail mix that we brought with us. We aren't letting this stop us."

Everyone relaxed at his words and helped themselves to the rations. They felt strength and resolve returning; everybody began to straighten and improve their posture. The Sages reported that they could still sense the direction of their goal but now its repugnance had diminished. The soldiers were eating and drinking quietly and confidently. Sapphira came over grasping along the rope to stand near the young girl.

"Suzy, I sensed the frightening horror that you were feeling back there. If this is getting to be too much for you, call on me. I'll walk beside you and, if need be, carry you. Keep in mind that these horrors, though not real, can have a very real and profound effect on you. They can alter your view of what's real and even lock you in a state of immobility. They can drive you mad, totally insane."

Suzy smiled though her friend could not see it in the midst of this darkness. "I won't go insane, Sapphira. I've many defenses of my own against the powers of darkness. I appreciate your concern and having you near is comfort and support enough. Now I believe we can and must move on."

As Suzy prepared to leave, she looked around and observed that all of the adults looked refreshed and revitalized after their break. The soldiers again stood tall and ready for combat. Marlen looked ready to move ahead. The Sages were grim faced but filled with resolve. Suzy knew it was time to go on even though this next portion was going to be unpleasant.

The renewed journey was indeed very tough and most unpleasant. It was like walking on eggs, trying so hard to walk softly but never softly enough as a great weight dragged you down. It was like trying to climb a greased pole without getting a good grip. Worst of all was the sinking feeling, constantly being drawn further and further into the slime yet being lifted up so that the horror never went away. As she plodded on, Suzy began to recite the words of Psalm 23 and when she came to 'walking through the valley of the shadow of death', she really understood what it meant. Still, the words encouraged her as she struggled on.

The menace was now very near - it poured out its venomous hatred towards her for resisting its repulsive terror. She glanced; the others were struggling and continuing only through extreme effort. *We have to stop. We need to use a different strategy, if we want to succeed.*

-25-

Timmy rolled over and lay in his bedroll looking at the burned out remains of the campfire. He jumped to his feet realizing that he had slept well into the morning. The sun beat down on him warmly and though he knew they did not need a campfire to keep them warm, a fire was necessary for cooking. He noticed a few glowing coals left from the large logs he had placed on the fire the night before. Choosing the right materials helped him coax a small fire into existence.

"Good morning." Timmy saw Tasha getting up as well.

"Oh my, I guess I really slept in this morning. The sun felt so warm that it was easy to stay curled up in bed." Tasha stretched and tossed her covers to the side.

"I see you have a fire started. I'll get some water so we can wash up and cook some porridge." She gathered some clothing, picked up two small containers that served as water buckets and walked off towards the stream. Tasha disappeared from view as she went behind the stone shed.

Timmy continued to nurture his fire and then dug through the packs to find some ground meal. This can be mixed with water and cooked into porridge. Here's some dried leaves with a minty scent that will make a tea. I'll have to wait for the water that Tasha's bringing.

In the meantime, he decided to scout out the area for any remaining evidence of the attackers from the night before. He put on his scabbard and drew the sword. *Good, that's ready.* He put the weapon away. *Now I can do check over the campsite and the area around it.* Timmy noticed Tasha returning with the water.

He called out to her. "I put out some tea leaves and the grain meal for porridge. It's next to the pot." She waved an acknowledgement.

Timmy continued his investigations. Soon, he was striding away from the camp following the trail left by the retreating attackers. He decided he had seen enough - besides he was hesitant to go far from the camp with Tasha left behind. As he turned to go back, Timmy spotted a shiny object nestled in the grass. He reached down to pick it up only to feel a tingling pain begin in his hand as he approached the object. He tried repeatedly and the pain intensified as his fingers drew near the item. He withdrew his hand, knelt down looked at mystery object. It appeared to be a button or a coin.

Timmy whistled to get Tasha's attention. When she looked his way, he called out. "Bring a small pot or a spoon to pick up a small object."

Tasha picked up a large spoon and one of the now empty water containers. She walked over to where he stood. He pointed to the grass. She saw the shiny objected and reached out with her hand.

"Be careful." Timmy placed his hand before her. "When I tried to pick it up, pain started in my fingers and shot up my arm. I don't think you should try it. Use the spoon to pick it up."

Tasha paused, looked at the spoon and then back at the small object. Ignoring his suggestion Tasha reached for the disk. She closed her hand over it and gently picked it out of the grass. It felt cool and damp in her hand. Timmy looked astonished; in fact, he had cringed as she reached for it. Tasha held it up to look at it.

It was hard to focus on it because the sun reflected so brightly off its shiny surface. She turned away from the sun so the disk was now in her shadow. It was still very bright but the side towards her displayed the image of a dagger with a serpent wrapped around it. She looked up at Timmy who frowned at the sight of the image. She turned it over to find the reverse side was blank. She looked closely at what appeared to be some slight grooves but they didn't seem to indicate anything to her. Timmy continued to frown but he didn't say anything. Tasha placed the disk in the water container.

Tasha looked at Timmy. "What was all that about? Were you just testing me, or what? I certainly didn't feel any pain."

"No, Tasha, I won't do that to you. From now on, I'll be straight with you and I expect the same in return. When I reached for the disk, I felt pain in my fingers even before I came close to touching it."

Tasha looked puzzled. "Why not try it again now that I have picked it up from the ground and placed it in the bucket?"

"My thoughts exactly! I will try it." He reached into the container; intense pain spread through his fingers and up his arm. Try as he might he couldn't bring his hand in contact with the disk. He withdrew his hand slowly; the pain eased away. He flexed his fingers. *My hand's a bit tender even though the pain's gone away.*

"Well I won't be trying that again. It's strange but then again this is Gorn. Things don't behave like they do back at home." Timmy continued to flex his fingers.

Tasha flashed a grin. "So, I have one over you after all." They both laughed at this and Tasha continued, "Let's get back and have some breakfast."

As they were finishing their breakfast, chatting about the valley, the food and the birds singing, a loud, painful wail that echoed through the valley and reverberated off the hills interrupted their conversation. They looked towards the castle as the screaming became more intense and shrill; suddenly, it stopped. Timmy jumped to his feet, checking his weapons and setting aside his bowl. Tasha, on seeing Timmy swing into action, quickly put on her sword. She knew they were about to go into action.

"What was that?" Tasha snapped her belt into place.

"Emeralda, we need to hurry."

Timmy walked over to the stone shed. He looked back at the castle. *I wonder what that scream was about. I'm sure it was Emeralda and she sounded like she was in great pain.* "We'll go this way simply because I've never scouted the entrance to the castle over there. Time's precious now."

"So get going; you lead. I'll follow, so don't get too far ahead. Remember I haven't gone this way as you have."

Timmy nodded. Good girl. I'm glad you said that. I was only thinking about getting to Emeralda as fast as I can. I'd have rushed off without thinking about you keeping up. He knew the way and set off on a quick run through the tunnel since he knew how it operated, where it led, and where it came out. Tasha proved to be quick on her feet and stayed right behind him as he ran through the tunnel. He was surprised how quickly they covered the distance.

As they emerged from the final stairwell Timmy was pleased to see how brightly lit the castle was. Of course, it had been dark last night with only the light of the stars and a crescent moon to illuminate the interior. Now the full sunlight poured through the long narrow windows that rose from just above his height to the ceiling level of the rooms. As he stepped into the corridor, he noticed how absolutely still and quiet it was inside the castle.

He stole a glance at his partner. Tasha was looking around, taking in all her surroundings. She nodded, knowing he had just warned her to be prepared for any sudden unexpected moves.

No worries here. Timmy moved quietly down the hallway towards the room that held the lodestone. It was so quiet as to be unsettling. Timmy felt every nerve on edge as he wondered what had happened. *I know Emeralda's involved. I'm not even going to guess at what happened. We're so close that we'll see for ourselves.*

Timmy approached the doorway and came to a standstill, shocked by the sight before him. Tasha came up behind and looked past his motionless body into the stone room. A large gem with many facets, each perfectly sculpted and polished, reflecting all the light that fell on it sat on a pedestal. An aura of bluish light surrounded the lodestone; Tasha knew this halo would be the force field that kept the stone safe. It was a sight so beautiful that her eyes were riveted to it.

"Emeralda! Emeralda, what's happened? Are you all right?" Timmy choked as he spoke.

Tasha's attention switched from the beauty of the lodestone to the pile of clothing lying before the pedestal. She stared at the disarray, suddenly comprehending that the mound was actually their guide, their foe, Emeralda. "Oh my goodness! Is she still alive?"

Tasha and Timmy ran over to where Emeralda lay on the floor. They stared at the pathetic, wizened old woman who had collapsed in the midst of what looked like a pile of rags. They couldn't believe her appearance - old and decrepit. Suddenly, she let out a breath that sounded more like a grunt. This rasping sound reassured Timmy and Tasha that for the time being she was still alive. Tasha couldn't believe how pathetic Emeralda appeared - that wild, energetic, self-centered witch who had captured and kidnapped them single-handedly now lay before them a physical wreck incapable of even moving.

Timmy came up beside the bundle and knelt down. He moved some of the clothing and groaned as he released her hands from the tangle. Tasha gasped at the sight before her. Emeralda's hands were a badly swollen, raw-red and burned combination of tortured flesh. Tasha turned her head away for a moment as she fought the urge to gag. However, she decided to take control of herself; Timmy, who obviously was trying to be rock solid, needed her in this time of crisis.

Tasha stepped forward and sat down near the stricken woman. Gently, she lifted Emeralda's head and placed it in her lap. She carefully moved the injured hands so she could cradle them in hers. The hands were raw, blistered, and feverish to the touch. As she touched them, she heard a low moan escape from Emeralda's lips.

Timmy was fascinated at how gently Tasha handled their injured foe, like one would treat a family member. *I'm certain I know what happened here. Emeralda's always talking about holding her baby in her arms. Why did I leave her alone with the lodestone? I should've known better. She's driven by a manic desire to caress and possess that stone*. Timmy shook his head. *I should've known the force field couldn't keep her away. Being in the presence of the stone and thus under its immediate influence she didn't have the willpower to resist the temptation to again cradle it. She put aside all memory of her last physical encounter with the lodestone - she must have reached out to touch and hold the stone. The consequences would have been immediate and dramatic. The surge of energy released on contact with the field and with the stone itself burned her deeply. She's fortunate to still be alive, likely because of her Sage nature*. Timmy knew she needed help and needed it right now. He reached out to remove her hands from Tasha and to take them in his.

Emeralda felt the fog thickening about her and felt herself slowly spinning in the prone position. She sensed a hot flush spreading over her body starting in her hands that burned with a deep and excruciating pain. Her beautiful child had initiated this pain when she had reached out to comfort it. As her hands encountered her baby, her little one had savagely bitten and refused to let go. The pain had been intense yet she felt such a great desire to remain in contact- an obsession almost. As the pain increased, Emeralda writhed between ecstasy and agony. She held on as long as she could bear but finally the pain overcame her. When she released her hold, she felt the pain subside but, in its place, a cold numbness spread throughout her body. She had experienced much the same earlier when she was paralyzed during the first encounter.

Emeralda was frightened because she knew how absolutely debilitating that had been and how much she had lost. Still, the desire to reach out for the stone had been so intense and the momentary bliss at possessing it even for the briefest of time overwhelmed all other fears and wishes. The seeming contradiction that her body was being consumed by a spreading chill at the exact same time as her hands were burning as if on fire didn't bother or concern her in the least.

Suddenly, she sensed a whispering, softly, cajolingly, sweetly urging her to let go, to sink into the fog and abandon all cares, worries, wants and desires, to be really free. The sounds were sweet, thick and syrupy, so honey-like as to be repugnant. Something drove a wedge through her heart and mind that tore at her very being. Deep down, her Sage nature and training churned into action, something that hadn't happened since before her cycles with the lodestone. A warm glow rose out of that stirring giving her a sensation of pleasure and well-being that she had missed for so long. She realized which voice was whispering to her. A wave of resistance and resolve rose within her in response to this soothing plea. She struggled to say something, to think of a rejection but her mind refused. She detected a subtle chuckle along with a cajoling message, "Its no use, Emeralda, you are mine. You can't escape me so let yourself go and submerge yourself in my goodness and sweetness. Ease yourself back. Let go."

Emeralda mused amid warm heat and icy chill, between luscious desire and wavering resolve, and wondered what she should do. She could feel her grip on reality slipping ever so slightly, yet slipping indeed. She dreaded the result but knew she couldn't prevent her loss of control; her strength was almost gone. At that moment, she felt she was completely losing the battle she was trained to fight as she slipped deeper into the fog.

All of a sudden, Emeralda felt hands holding hers pulling her free of the abyss into which she was tumbling. The chill was dissipating rapidly while the agonizing heat in her hands subsided slowly but surely. The sticky sweetness and the horrid slime were gone. The sweet whispers were replaced by fanatical shrieks demanding her to let go and to obey intermingled with curses of disgust and demeaning characterization. She felt her strength returning, although she couldn't explain it. With the return of her strength, she felt a deepening calmness.

As she relaxed, Emeralda opened her eyes to find her head resting in Tasha's lap and her hands enclosed by Timmy's. Her first reaction was simply to settle deeper into Tasha's lap and to relinquish control of her hands to Timmy. She was somewhat surprised by this out of character reaction yet did nothing to upset the calmness washing over her. She smiled at her benefactors.

That smile took Tasha by complete surprise. Of course, she was astonished that Emeralda could respond in that way but also by the stunning beauty of that smile. She could hardly believe the incredible transformation in Emeralda. Before her lay, a beautiful, mature woman who showed strength and conviction and whose green eyes sparkled with delight. Tasha found herself catching her breath at the stunning sight and had to consciously will herself to breathe and remain calm.

Timmy's amazement was just as great; he had never expected such a change to occur. His eyes remained riveted on this beautiful Sage who so incredibly looked like Sapphira. He had known all along they were sisters but had never really seen any likeness. Now, as the rough and ragged edges melted away a very wise and beautiful person was emerging. Her smile was so uplifting that Timmy found it hard to concentrate and hold on to her rapidly healing hands.

"So, young prince," Emeralda spoke softly, "you indeed are full of surprises- wise, gracious, tactical, and a healer as well. I'm certain that there's much more about you that you haven't yet revealed."

Emeralda smiled in appreciation and closed her eyes, nestling her head in the lap that held her. She hadn't felt this good for so long and she was enjoying it. The warmth of Timmy's hands spread throughout her body as she felt the healing continue. The comfort of Tasha's sweet embrace filled with a gentleness that she realized she had been missing for far too long. Memories of contentment, friendship and sisterly love came flooding back with such intensity that her eyes filled rapidly and little rivers of tears trickled down her cheeks. Emeralda felt Tasha gently dabbing them with the corner of her sleeve. She felt wonderful.

Timmy and Tasha continued to be amazed, as they watched the many changes taking place in Emeralda. Both felt a deep sense of joy that they were present and had a role to play in this miracle. Sensing his job was complete Timmy slowly rose to his feet without releasing Emeralda's hands. He gave her a gentle pull and Emeralda opened her eyes, smiled and slowly rose to her feet, reluctantly leaving the softness and warmth of Tasha's lap yet somewhat excited to experience her surroundings. Her eyes left Timmy and turned towards the lodestone.

She felt sadness for a moment but then she smiled. Tasha had risen to her feet to stand next to Timmy. Both had a look of concern on their faces as they watched Emeralda gaze towards the lodestone. Their show of concern touched Emeralda. "I sense that the force field is still in place despite my attempt to interrupt it. As such, the stone is safe from outside attack. I've just cast a search spell and don't detect any enemies nearby presently although I do sense that someone has been here recently."

Both of the young people relaxed as Emeralda spoke, now realizing that they were dealing with a radically changed person. Tasha grimaced as she turned to Emeralda. "Yes, last night while you were here with the lodestone, two bandits or scouts entered our camp and tried to capture me. Timmy came after them with his sword waving in the air, like a glowing torch, and scared them off."

Emeralda nodded. "So it does that for you. I guess I shouldn't be surprised since you are truly a gifted prince. It doesn't glow for everyone."

Timmy smiled and pointed towards Tasha. "It glows for Tasha as well."

Emeralda raised her eyebrows at this information. *I would never have expected that. I wonder what it means.*

Timmy continued. "It becomes very heavy for her. Though it glows for her she can't wield it, much like I can't swing hers with the ease she does."

Emeralda pursed her lips. "This is very interesting. It would appear as though we may be seeing one of your limitations, fair prince. Now you, young lady, I call you princess. Obviously you have talents that we've yet to discover."

"I believe there's more. We'll show you when we return to the camp. We've a token from the intruders that we want you to see." Timmy stood up and started towards the hallway.

"Well, let's go back to the camp now. The two of you are likely hungry and I can see that the stone is safe and secure." Emeralda turned and walked out into the hallway without hesitation and without looking back.

Timmy and Tasha shrugged but didn't say anything as they followed her down the hallway to a set of large doors. Emeralda pushed them open and the valley scene spread out before them. They were standing in the main entrance to the castle; before them lay a path leading down to the stone shed and their small encampment.

They stood there looking out, admiring the beauty of the valley. Tasha gazed at the sky. "The sun's nearing the western horizon. We've spent the entire day inside this castle and somehow I never sensed timc was passing."

Timmy nodded his head. "Nor I. I thought it'd be high noon at the latest."

Emeralda again smiled to her companions. "You spent much more time healing me than you imagined. I'm very grateful that you'd take the time and the effort as well as the risk to help me. Thank you so very much."

Timmy and Tasha smiled in appreciation at what Emeralda had just said. They followed her down the path to the camp. Tasha walked over to the container that held the disk they had found earlier in the day. She picked it up and held it in her hand to show Emeralda. Emeralda frowned at the sight of it; the bright sparkle she displayed earlier now replaced by a look of deep sadness.

"A button of the dark lord. So! His minions have come this close. I can't touch it; quite frankly I don't even wish to look at it anymore." Emeralda turned away and began to put a few food items together for a meal.

Tasha was about to say something but she noticed that Timmy was shaking his head. She nodded and placed the disk in her pocket. *Strange, it doesn't affect me yet these two want nothing to do with it. Well, I'll just hold on to it for a while longer.*

Everyone pitched in preparing the supper meal. All had plenty to think about so they passed their time in silence.

-26-

Suzy found a rocky spot to stop for a rest. This allowed the members of the team to sit down for some relief from the gruelling march. She led each of them to a rock to sit on since they were unable to see in the darkness. When she completed this task, she found a seat next to Sapphira who placed a hand on her shoulder; that gentle touch lifted all the tension of her struggle.

Suzy spoke softly to her friend. “I think we’ve come as far as we can as a group. It appears as though the strength’s being sucked out of everyone.”

“It doesn’t help that we’re also dealing with an intrusion on the lodestone. That’s really dragging us down. We can’t concentrate on the repulsive nature of this task.”

“What sort of problem is happening at the lodestone?” Suzy stretched and placed her hands behind her head. “Does it have anything to do with Emeralda?”

Sapphira sighed. “Yes, of course it does. She’s in the presence of the lodestone, as we speak. We feel a battle going on as she struggles with her desire for the stone and her deep fear of the consequences of actually having it. It’s only a matter of time until she’s overwhelmed by that desire. I can only hope that she won’t be injured too seriously because we don’t have anyone to go to her at this critical time.”

"She has Timmy with her. He has healing powers which should prove to be useful given the fact that she will be injured."

"If she lets him help." Sapphira whispered and bowed her head.

"Well, right now we have a different problem to deal with. We're very close to whatever's in this darkness. I can feel its presence not only in my mind but also with my skin. I have goose bumps and chilblains. The Sages are preoccupied with protecting the lodestone and Emeralda. As such they're a hindrance in proceeding. The soldiers are walking blind and may be wonderful fighters but they must be able to see their foe. Only I have my sight and the ability to move around obstacles as we continue on this trek."

Sapphira was quick to respond. "I think I know where you're going with this and it has some merit. However, you need a Sage because we can sense the direction to go to reach our goal; we won't be sent off by a false lead. Although you think the soldiers are blind, they aren't incapable. You need a guard. Besides, I suspect the soldiers won't be left behind."

"I know that. We must leave quickly. Whatever's out there needs to be dealt with as soon as possible. The soldiers under Blog's command are exposed to the army of Natas. I think we should leave within ten minutes."

"In that case, young princess, you've just enough time to have some soldier drink and rations. You may think that you don't need them but you are facing a situation, which is going to require all the strength you can muster. I'll join you in this snack since I'll be travelling with you." Sapphira reached for her pack.

I'm pleased that Sapphira's coming along as my guide. She's given me strength up to now and I know I can rely on her to help me. Suzy reached into her pack to get some of her rations as Sapphira did the same. Suzy was certain that her friend really didn't need those rations but was simply being friendly. Still, Suzy was happy that she was with her.

Marlen turned towards Suzy and Sapphira. "So you've decided to go on your own. That's the right decision under the circumstances. I'll stay with Gelder and Burgan to assist in strengthening the force field. We'll also divert our wills to help you by following Sapphira. Unfortunately, we can't mindlink so close to the enemy since he'd sense and use it to spy on our efforts. Suzy, you're facing the biggest challenge of your life to this point. You need to call on all your strength and you must allow Sapphira to help. You're going to be making a decision that'll be difficult. You'll be losing something you value a great deal. Of course, we know that you'll be rewarded and we hope that'll be sufficient. Don't ask me to explain because I can't. Even if I could, I wouldn't when we're this close to the enemy. I only wish I could be there with you but I can't."

Suzy took another mouth of the wonderful juice; *That's so refreshing. No wonder soldiers take it with them on their long marches or into stiff battles.* She packed up her small sack of rations and put them away noticing that Sapphira was doing the same. She placed her pack in position and watched as the soldiers quickly stood, ready to accompany her on this part of the journey. Suzy knew they would not leave her side even if she were to order it. Suzy prepared a short rope with four loops. Each member of this new group took hold of the rope and started following her. Sapphira walked directly behind Suzy so she could whisper encouragement and place a hand on her shoulder for direction and for support. The two soldiers walked brusquely with their free hands on the hilt of their sheathed swords.

Suzy marched on into the mist, deliberately picking her path among the boulders that lay about on the ground in this portion of the desert. She had to be mindful of her unseeing companions. Her concentration helped her deflect the undulating surges of dread that kept sweeping over her. Wave after wave of horrid sensations smashed against the beachhead of her mind. In the midst of all of this, she felt very cold and ached primarily in her legs. Suzy kept staring straight ahead looking for something unusual. The whispering continued to bombard her mind. She wasn't hearing these sounds with her ears, which were picking up the slow crunch of their march. Sometimes the whispers would swell into wails of pain or choruses of heckling. Suzy didn't understand a word that was said but she felt the intent behind all the voices.

She felt Sapphira's hand rest on her shoulder; Suzy knew she was in good hands. She allowed her mind to go back to those wonderful lessons that Timmy and she had studied. She recited Psalm 121 and felt uplifted by the knowledge that she could always receive help.

Silly girl. A voice echoed in her mind. You've no business here. Go back home where you can recite any poem you like. Here in Gorn there's no need to call for help like that. Here in Gorn everyone's free to act as he or she chooses. Here we don't need to sing praises to some hidden deity or call out to the Creator. Go home, little girl.

Suzy shook her head. She was aware that this change in language was a clear indication of how desperate the enemy was. She had to move on and not allow herself to be distracted.

Home, girl, home! A new voice shouted through her mind. Isn't that where your mother is. She's probably looking for you right now, worried as all good mothers are.

Suzy moved on determined not to let these voices change her mind. As she did she felt as if she was up to her neck in freezing, stinking slime. Suzy wanted to vomit but again a gentle reassuring hand on her shoulder called her back to her task.

A shrieking voice caught her attention. You aren't listening, little fool. You can't do anything here. If you don't leave at once, both your mother and father are in grave danger. Don't be fooled by Sages who have their own agenda to follow. They don't care about you; if they did, they wouldn't be sending you through this slime field on a venture over which you haven't a chance of succeeding. Go home. Just because your mother's a princess doesn't make the danger for her any less as you so foolishly march on. Turn around. Don't let that blue witch cast her spell over you. You must save yourself and your parents.

These thoughts were so venomous and grotesque they made her shiver. She groaned as she thought about her mother. *Am I really exposing her to an immediate danger*? Suzy worried a moment. Then she recalled the instruction she had learned. "Stand firm," she whispered, knowing that she had all the help she needed.

She felt Sapphira's warm hand on her shoulder. Radiating from that touch, she felt a warm assurance spreading throughout her shivering body. Her necklace seemed to be sending her a signal in the form of a slight vibration and a quiet jingling sound. Suzy lifted her right hand to her neck and felt the crystals; the spherical gem was responsible for these experiences.

Just before her, as wave after wave of nightmarish torments broke over her consciousness amplified with loathsome wailing and a cacophony of horrid shrieking, Suzy detected a glowing spot within a few paces. Her feet seemed planted in gumbo and as heavy as lead. Her legs screamed with pain yet the warmth of Sapphira's hand continued to drive back the bone chilling numbness of the ever-thickening slime that had slowed her progress. Her breathing was rapid and shallow; Suzy could feel faintness overcoming her. She gripped the necklace and willed herself onward, reassured by the determined effort the dark lord was making. She had to keep on because he was trying too hard to stop her. *Run the good race*, Suzy prayed as she took strong steps to bring herself along side the glowing object.

Before her, Suzy saw a roughly sculpted rock in the form of a goat's head. It was entirely black obsidian but one spot was emitting a bright glow. This beam of light contained all the hideous grotesque antipathy in an attempt to overcome the group as they approached. Sapphira raised every mental barrier she had learned as a Sage to block these messages, yet some filtered through to burn in her mind. The soldiers were being torn apart by the images that they were witnessing but their discipline and training allowed them to march on. The dogged determination of the little princess inspired both Sage and soldiers to carry on.

Suzy scrutinized the rough goat's face to discover that the bright spot was the left eye of the sculpture. She moved her hand over the opening noting its size. She worked her fingers over the right eye determining the dimensions and its actual size. She again felt a tingle on her neck and she reached up to grasp the spherical gem in her fingers. At once, Suzy realized the gem was exactly the size of the eye socket, that opening from which all the hideous wrath was spewing. She removed her necklace from her neck. *I think I know what needs to be done here.*

Are you ready for this, sweet Suzy*?* A new voice spoke softly within her mind.

Oh, what a change! Now the voice is charming and soothing. Where are all the shouts and curses? Sure a change - no little girl. It actually called me by my name. Careful Suzy. She closed her fingers over the gems.

Oh Suzy, you don't have to be careful around me. I just want you to think about what you're planning. That necklace of yours has meant so much to you. Remember how you used it in the past to get so much. All of it was for good just as you always try so hard to do. If you put that gem in the socket of this stone, you will forever lose it. It's part of the entire necklace. What kind of necklace will you have if it's missing one of the gems? This crystal helped defeat the dark commander. Do you really want to be without such an important treasure? You deserve to have it all the time.

Suzy stood with her hand over the face deep in thought. Memories flooded back as she recalled the first time she had used the awesome power of these crystals to free the Sages from their prison. She remembered how the crystals had helped her to free the dark land of the plague that covered the region. She recalled how the dark commander had hesitated when she had held up her crystals and how they had banished him to some dark limbo. Suzy liked the feel of the necklace in her hand.

Suzy felt Sapphira again place her hand on her shoulder. This time she resented the intrusion into her thoughts. She wanted to relish her control of the crystals and to reminisce about the wonderful times she had had using them. They had come to her – they were meant for her. She reached over and took Sapphira's hand away from her shoulder.

You see, Suzy, the Sages are just trying to use you. They resent the fact that you were given control over the crystals. They long for the use of them. However, it's you who has the crystals and it's you who should always have them around her neck. The voice was sweet and cajoling.

The soothing conversation mesmerized Suzy; however, she wondered why she was being told things that she knew to be untrue. *The Sages can't use the crystals because they were meant for ordinary people. After all, I am an ordinary person and I enjoy having the crystals.*

The sweet voice cut in again and crooned. Hold on to what you have, Suzy. If you keep these crystals where they belong, around your neck, I promise you'll never regret the decision. Many wonderful things will come your way, least of all, power over many lands.

Now Suzy became uncomfortable: she was beginning to realize what was happening to her. *I'm being tempted and I'm allowing it to happen. The crystals are meant for good and not for my pleasure. I've been given a wonderful thing to care for until the time comes for me to give it away. Marlen warned me about losing something I cherish; now I understand what he was talking about. Oh, my gosh. I've forgotten Blog, who's out there on the front lines facing the enemy, and Timmy, who's in the hands of Emerulda. Here I am wondering about what was best for me.*

She reached back to find Sapphira's hand poised just above her shoulder. Suzy gently placed it back on her shoulder and gave it a couple of love pats. *I know I'm going to have some regrets but I have a duty to perform.* She moved the gem near the opening.

Please, Suzy, think about what you're about to lose. Your beautiful set of crystals won't be complete. You'll forever regret making such a selfish move when you had a better choice. Just move on. Go back to where you belong. The sweetest voice yet to speak tried to persuade her. Place the gem back around your neck where it rightfully belongs. It makes you look so beautiful.

Suzy considered for a moment and again the phrase 'Stand firm' came to mind. She plunged the spherical gem into the empty socket. Just before she completed her deed, a wave of fiery hatred engulfed her, accompanied by a scream. You'll be sorry. You're losing the entire necklace because of this, you fool. You could've had so much if only you'd have bowed... agggghhhh!

The goat's face lit up briefly and then shuddered. The earth trembled slightly and the darkness slackened. It began to break up and the late afternoon sunshine began to filter through. Suzy looked down at her spherical crystal to see it had blackened deeper than the obsidian face. She unfastened the gem from her necklace and then replaced the remaining jewels around her neck. It felt strange - incomplete; she knew without a doubt she had just lost something very precious.

Suzy found herself in the embrace of her beaming friend. She allowed herself to sink into those arms in appreciation; she knew this phase of the adventure was over. The soldiers clapped her on the back, wishing her congratulations for her victory. Suzy beamed at the triumph she had just achieved but deep down she felt guilty that she had taken so long to do what was right.

"You were wonderful, my friend," Sapphira said quietly. "You've done such a beautiful thing. I know the cost of it, my dear. You made it seem so easy. You remembered I was here by you all the time. You just reached out when you felt the need."

"Oh, Sapphira, it wasn't easy. It should have been but I was almost taken in by that sweet talk. I feel just terrible about that."

"It's never easy to stand firm, Suzy. The most important part of what you just said was that you were almost taken in. Almost taken in isn't the same as being taken in. Don't beat yourself up for thinking. Now look over there! The Sages and Marlen are coming."

Marlen held out his arms and Suzy sprinted into them. She was happy that they were all together again and that they could see. Marlen held her back and beamed, "We were right about bringing you out here. You are a remarkable, young woman. Without a doubt, you are a princess. Now, let's see what you were up against."

Sapphira, Marlen, Gelder and Burgan went forward to see what had caused this problem. They stood looking at the obsidian face and their expressions displayed deep concern. The soldiers, however, paid the sculpture no attention and congratulated Suzy again. They snapped to attention and gave her a salute; she returned the gesture, much to their delight. Then she moved over to where the Sages were standing.

Marlen wrapped an arm around her. "So you had to battle a rogue stone, my dear."

"A rogue stone? What exactly is a rogue stone?"

"A thing of evil designed by an evil master, the dark lord himself. It's an imitation of the lodestone. When the Sages created the lodestone to concentrate our powers in the battle against the forces of darkness, Natas made imitations of it. He stored some of his power and strength within them. He sacrificed the lives of many to transfer their power to these rogues. I see that you've made a great sacrifice - I recognize that left eye. You indeed were called on to give up something of great value to you." He gathered her into his arms to hug her.

Suzy suddenly felt tired and weak. She trembled but Marlen held on to her. He looked up at his companions. "I think we need to set up camp here for a short while. We're all very tired and in need of nourishment. After we rest, we can begin our return march. In the meantime, we need to be watchful in our preparations; the enemy knows his stone has failed. He also knows we must be here so we must guard against being ambushed."

Suzy wanted to help but felt too tired to move. She relaxed in Marlen's arms as he sat down on a boulder. She closed her eyes, felt a deep sense of sadness and then allowed sleep to sweep over her.

-27-

The sun had gone down, the evening meal eaten and the dishes cleaned. The campfire burned brightly as Timmy added some logs in preparation for the night. The three sat staring into the fire, each dwelling on their own thoughts. Conversation had been very sparse since they returned to the campsite. Emeralda stretched and looked about, taking in the two young people. "I must apologize for being so quiet and withdrawn. I'm elated at being released from pain by your healing, young prince. As we left the castle I was looking forward to my new-found freedom. We came back to this place; I saw the disk. I was reminded of the dark one, of his insidious creeping and growing strength. It was like a kick in the stomach."

"Emeralda, I don't hold that against you and I'm sure Tasha doesn't either. We know there are times when everyone must have a little time for himself or herself. Oh, by the way, I'm tired of this 'prince' stuff. I'd like to be called Timmy. It's what my friends call me."

Tasha lifted her head and looked at Emeralda. "Timmy's said it well, Emeralda. Please call me Tasha. By the way if you feel up to it, I'd like to know more about the disk."

Tears formed in Emeralda's eyes; Timmy and Tasha were taken aback at her reaction. Emeralda's voice trembled as she spoke. "You want me to use your 'friend names' after all I've put you through, all the deceit and selfish ambitions that you were subjected to. That's not justice for you at all. In that case, I would appreciate you calling me Mera from now on."

Tasha smiled. "Mera. I like that. It has such a soft and friendly sound to it. Timmy and I don't want to get any revenge. We just want to be helpful now that you're recovering."

"I see that and I don't deserve it. However, you asked about the disk and I will tell you what I know about it, which unfortunately isn't much. It seems to be a communication device for the dark lord to remain in touch with his followers. I'm not sure how it works but it provides him with information concerning the whereabouts of his minions."

Tasha shivered as she heard this explanation. She reached into her pocket and brought forth the disk. It lay cold and unappealing in the palm of her hand. She stared at the serpent image. "I'll throw this away immediately. I don't need any dark lord following me around."

"It's not that easy, I'm afraid. First, I don't believe you're in any danger since you aren't a follower of Natas." Tasha shook her head emphatically in agreement with this. Emeralda continued, "However, we can't leave it here in this valley so close to the lodestone. It may draw the dark lord to this location. It seems as though those two intruders may have followed us in, even as we marched. I wasn't careful enough to spot them. We can only hope that their presence here wasn't monitored by Natas."

Tasha looked again at the disk and although not completely assured she put the device back in her pocket.

Timmy looked up. "It'll soon be time to go to sleep. What's our plan now, Emer..., I mean Mera? I suppose I'll need some time to get used to a different name for you."

"As I will in getting used to walking away from the lodestone. It's safe where it is. I wasn't concerned about its security, Timmy. You were right all along when you said I simply wanted it for myself. Please help me when I slip back as I'm sure I will. It still calls out to me."

Tasha patted Emeralda's hand. "We're here to support you, especially when you're feeling the strain of being away from the lodestone."

"Timmy, you asked what we do next. I'm going to take you away from here - back to where we originally came into Gorn. Then I can take you home as I've promised."

"Good. In the morning, we can be on our way. I think the fire's burning at the right level so let's turn in and get some sleep." Timmy poked the fire with a stick.

"Sounds good to me." Tasha stood up. "It's been quite a day."

They washed up and prepared for sleep. Each then slipped into their sleeping covers and quickly Tasha was sound asleep. Timmy closed his eyes but sleep did not come immediately. He lay there thinking about all the events that had taken place since leaving home. *I find it fascinating that I was able to heal Emeralda's terrible burn. She is, after all, a Sage, a special person with deep knowledge, hidden strengths and powers.* Timmy opened his eyes and looked at the burning log before closing his eyes again. *I wonder why that disk bothered me the way it did. Oh, and there's Tasha's sword – that was weird. Nothing like this has happened to me before. Maybe Emeralda, ah, Mera's right: this maybe one of the limitations I have here in Gorn. No bother, I know I have weaknesses, truth be told, many of them. I'll just have to keep them in mind, maybe, even work a little harder.*

There were so many unusual questions; he did not have his best friend to talk with about his concerns. He wondered what Suzy was doing back at home. Did she know he'd come to Gorn? No, probably she didn't even miss him since all these days in Gorn were likely no more than a few minutes. *What's really interesting is that first night hasn't yet passed. I can go back and haven't missed a thing.* Timmy continued to ponder the events that had taken place, as sleep seemed to elude him.

Emeralda had closed her eyes and at once drifted into a tranquil state of happiness and euphoria. She began to remember many of the delightful events of her earlier years. She remembered the great times she enjoyed with Sapphira as they had studied and trained to become Sages. She was so relaxed and at peace that her body felt a warm glow. Suddenly, a dark cloud passed overhead from which came a loathsome scream. A cold dark fog rolled into her peaceful home and again she felt herself falling into an abyss. This was all too familiar and even though it was deja vu all over again, Emeralda began to whimper and groan. She wanted to be free of this nightmare and able to enjoy the sunlight that had come into her life. She grasped at anything that would slow or stop this agonizing plunge into a desolate unknown. Her breathing became erratic and her heart beat rapidly. Emeralda tried to close her mind to this and desperately tried to awaken from such a hideous dream. Voices spoke to her in rounds admonishing her for feeling such peace when she had done so much evil. Other voices warned her that she would never feel any joy. More voices threatened her for trying to escape the clutches of darkness, ridiculing her for thinking she could ever again be free to enjoy the goodness and splendour of life. A cacophony of jeering, laughing, sneering and shrieking filled her mind; she fought off an urge to vomit even though she knew she would not. Her body was racked with undulations of pain, pressure, hot and cold; she writhed from the torture to which she was being afflicted. “Please help me,” she whispered.

Emeralda felt herself drawn up by a strong pair of hands with a firm grip on her. She opened her eyes to find herself looking into the semi-lit face of Timmy who was holding her by the shoulders. His face was etched with deep concern.

“Mera, Mera! This all has to come to an end. You can’t continue to suffer like this every night.”

“Oh Timmy, if that were only possible but I don’t think I shall ever be free of this torment. My life has been so chaotic and filled with evil; now I must suffer the consequences.”

“Nonsense, Mera. You’re sick and it’s no wonder, considering how deeply the lodestone wounded you. No one knew the effects of a prolonged exposure to that rock of power but you were subjected to it. Now, some of those effects still linger, having a tremendous grip on you.”

Tasha had come over to Emeralda’s side. She had awakened when she heard the conversation and knew the Sage was in need of someone to provide her comfort. Tasha placed her arm around Emeralda and was rewarded by a very grateful smile and by the resting of a head on her shoulder.

“You have been deeply injured that it afflicts your mind,” Tasha whispered soothingly.

“I know that’s true but I can’t do anything about it. The Sages tried but they couldn’t help me.” Mera wore a pained expression.

“Maybe Timmy can help you. “

“I don’t know. If the Sages together couldn’t, maybe Timmy can’t by himself either.”

Timmy considered this for a moment, rubbing his hands together. “I really want to try, Mera. I don’t consider myself equal to the Sages but there’s one major difference this time. When the Sage council treated you, you had a firm desire to resist, to stay in contact with the stone, even to possess it as a child. All of those proved too much for the Sages’ attempts to bring about a healing. Now you’ve a chance to let all that go and come out cleansed - healed of a terrible injury that plagues you whenever you’re trying to rest.”

“But Timmy, how do you know that I’ve let the stone go completely? Even I don’t know that I have for sure. Do you remember how I stared at the stone after you healed me? I could still hear it crying out to me. I didn’t respond as I had in the past because I was enjoying the freedom and peace that you were responsible for. Can you be sure that I’ve changed, really changed, that I’m ready to be healed?”

Tasha cradled Mera’s head next to hers. “You’ve come so far, dear Mera. Both Timmy and I can see how changed you are. Sure, it’s only been a few hours but we never expected to see even this much. Now, it really comes down to you. Timmy shouldn’t attempt to heal you unless you’re prepared to accept the change as permanent. That means that you must be willing to release the stone, that you’re going to give up all claim to the stone and that the cries don’t really exist but are produced within yourself as part of your desire to hold and control the lodestone.”

Timmy released Mera’s shoulders and stepped back. “I can’t order you to be healed; that’s your choice to make. I’m willing to attempt a healing but only if you’re just as willing.”

“You two are too good to be real; much too good for me, that’s for sure. I’ve suffered like this for so long that I almost believe it’s normal. Almost - I said, because for the past few hours I've experienced peace, joy and delightful memories such that I don't want any of it to end. When we came back here the sight of the disk showed me that Natas is still hard at work and that my desire for the stone hasn't ended. So what should I do? I know what I want more than ever. I want to let my obsession for the lodestone go because this short time of freedom and bliss has reawakened in me a desire to be the Sage I trained to be. I want that part of my old life back even if I can never completely get it all back. You need a definite answer, dear friends; this is it. I want to be free of these longings; I want to be free of all this suffering. I want to be healed."

Timmy smiled in response to this answer. "I'll do all I can for you, Mera. You're putting yourself in my hands and no matter what happens please remain fixed on this process. The same goes for you, Tasha. I don't know what'll happen so I ask you to stay with me through all that happens."

Tasha nodded, "I'll do whatever's needed. I think we should have Mera lie down and I'll cradle her head in my lap as we did during the earlier healing. I need my covers over my shoulders because the night air has a definite chill to it."

Timmy looked around. "I'll bring my covers here as well in case they're needed. I'm also going to add some more wood to our campfire and I think we should have a drink of water, each of us. I then want to have a few moments to myself to prepare for this."

He rose and walked over to his sleeping roll. He brought both his and Tasha's covers to the two women who were rearranging their positions. He then added three larger logs to the campfire. He picked up a water jug and brought it over after pouring himself a drink. He then retreated to the other side of the fire, knelt down, and bowed his head. He remained in that position for several minutes.

His companions drank some water and then settled in, waiting for him to be ready. Mera smiled at Tasha, "Thanks for helping me. I really don't deserve it after all I did to you earlier. But I guess you already know this since you and Timmy have the ability to read minds…."

Tasha interrupted her with a hearty laugh. Timmy opened his eyes as Tasha laughingly said to him, "Timmy, did you hear that? Our dear friend here believes you and I can read minds."

Timmy laughed when he heard this. "There are times when that would be very useful but then there are times when I don't want to know what others are thinking."

"But you two were able to do so much together. You seemed to know what each other was going to do next."

"That was all part of an act, Mera, to throw you off track and to add confusion in a situation where we knew we were almost helpless. I suppose we ought to apologize for our deceit now that we're becoming friends. We need to be honest, to trust each other fully in all that we do." Timmy bowed his head.

"I too want to say that I'm sorry that I had to mislead you like I did earlier in our journey. I really was injured but Timmy healed me. After that, I pretended that I'd never been hurt."

"I appreciate you telling me the truth. This is all so new to me. I've lived a lie for so very long."

"Oh, Timmy, I'm sorry I interrupted you just now. You wanted some time to prepare and I just had to laugh. It seemed so funny." Tasha blushed and placed her right hand over her mouth.

"It's okay," Timmy said as he rose to his feet. "Actually, I am ready; this chance to laugh has made me relax. Now, I feel that I can begin at once."

Timmy came over and knelt beside Emeralda. He put his left hand on her head and breathed very slowly as he closed his eyes. He allowed himself to relax, concentrating on his task. Mera too closed her eyes as she relaxed. Tasha alone kept her eyes open as she watched the effects on her friends; she also kept watch over the valley.

Timmy found himself walking down a long hallway that reminded him of the corridor in the nearby castle. As he walked down its length, a mist was forming along the floor; as he neared a doorway the large door would swing open, the interior of the room would brighten, and the light would spill into the hallway. However, as he moved the mist would thicken and deepen. At first, it was just a wisp along the floor; it had now grown to knee height. Moreover, it was resisting his movement. *I have never experienced anything like this when I've healed in the past. I just placed my hand on the person and the healing took place. Even my earlier healing of Emeralda wasn't like this.*

He thought about what was happening and it seemed as though Mera was opening all the doors of her mind. As each room opened, the hidden recesses revealed their secret contents. Light flooded into the dark confines of her life. As he ventured farther down the hallway, his probing became more difficult to do. The fog intensified and the corridor became darker and darker. Still, the doors continued to open but the light within wasn't having much effect in the corridor. He was having difficulty moving forward because walking through this fog was like walking through sticky ooze. This mass of slime was obscuring his view of the hallway down which he had to travel. *I want to carry on, to open all the hidden nooks of my friend's mind. Then and only then, Mera can finally be free.*

Timmy heard whispering all around him as he slowly moved. Some were sweet and enticing; others were demented and wailing. All at once, one voice was much clearer than all others, "Why are you here, fool? You've no business within these walls. This all belongs to me and, if you stay here, you must give me your allegiance or suffer the consequences for trespassing where you don't belong. Back out of here now and I'll pretend nothing's happened."

Timmy felt sick to his stomach after listening to that voice. His skin crawled and goose bumps sprang up all over his body. The hair on the back of his neck stood straight up. He could not see anything before him now, so deep had become the darkness around him.

Timmy found his free hand grasping his pouch around his neck. He used a finger to open the little bag and his fingers made contact with his bracelet. The coolness of the band felt wonderful to his touch. It gave him a sense of security as he faced the uncertainty of the darkness. *I wore this bracelet within the darkness before the hidden castle and was able to see. I need the band to continue my healing journey for this new friend.* He slipped his hand through the bracelet. Suddenly, the darkness surrounding him in the hallway was only a slight dimness.

Through the air in the corridor, black bat-like creatures flew by causing him to wince before he realized they were only thoughts projected at him to throw him off course. Again, voices assailed him with warnings and threats but now they grew more menacing and cold. Timmy ignored them and proceeded down the hall - more doors opened. At the end of the corridor stood a massive door; now a very chilling wind swept through the hall. He shivered as he was accosted by a sinister voice, "Get out while you can, young fool. You don't know the power you're up against. Do you think that this black witch really appreciates what you're doing? You're ruining her life by changing her. She's accepted my path and has enjoyed going that way. You'll just wreck everything that she's worked hard to set up. Leave this room as it is. It's mine. If you open it, you will suffer. Get out while you can."

Timmy moved to the door. It was locked. He looked around and again the voice railed at him. "You don't listen, do you? Get out, fool, because you can't win here. In fact, you'd do well to bow down before me; if you do, I'll make you rich, powerful and in charge of many nations."

"Stop right there. You've used that line before on one much greater than I. I won't bow before you for I bow only to my Lord. Be gone! You appear over and over under many different names but you're never any different."

In the silence that followed, Timmy examined the lock on the door. He saw a star-like symbol where there should have been a keyhole. He recognized the symbol; it was identical to the one on the door of the dungeon cell that had confined Marlen. Timmy felt the symbol again and he knew with certainty that it was the same. He laughed aloud. "Not much imagination, Old Nick. You didn't come up with a different lock because you lack any creativity. All you know is how to destroy and I won't be a part of that."

Timmy removed the bracelet from his wrist. Immediately, he was plunged back into darkness. His ears were filled with hideous cackling and jeers. He avoided concentrating on this noise and moved the band forward. Using his sense of touch, Timmy inserted the bracelet into the indentation that matched it on the door. Still the door refused to budge.

"Come on now, Mera, open up. You can't keep this last room closed. You must let it go," Timmy spoke loudly.

"Leave it alone, she won't let you in. I was in only once and then she closed it - even to me. Yes, I locked it so she'd never be able to clear it. You don't want it open for when it does open, you will be harmed. There's a price for interfering here where you don't belong; healing in the future will always bring pain, if you don't withdraw. Besides, Emeralda doesn't want it opened because then she'd have to abandon her greatest desire which is to hold the lodestone as her very own."

A lull followed this speech. Timmy didn't know what to do next so he waited, hoping that Mera would come through. Suddenly, the door began to open as he heard Mera say, "I want to be free."

A bright light poured out of the room and drove the darkness out of the corridor. A black mist hugging the floor flowed out of the room. As it slid past, Timmy discovered his legs first had a numbing sensation and then they burned with a horrible pain. He gasped as the mist continued to swirl about his legs. He had never felt anything so intense and found himself breathing rapidly. He saw that the room was clear so he pulled his bracelet from the door and removed his hand from Mera's head.

At once, the hallway vanished and he found himself looking into the faces of his companions. Mera was smiling, relaxing in Tasha's lap. Tasha flashed a grin and a-thumbs up signal. Timmy felt exhausted, noting the pain was gone. However, the memory of it was very vivid. He placed the bracelet back into the pouch, securing it around his neck.

Mera smiled again. "So what other hidden talents and trinkets do you possess? A special bracelet hidden from sight and the ability to vanish yet still be physically present along with a strong will and the determination to move on also thrown in for extras."

"I know I should've told you about the bracelet but there wasn't time to do so."

"Don't apologize, Timmy, the way I've treated you and my past record are reasons enough to keep those items secret for a long time. I feel honoured that you've allowed me to know you so well in such a short time. I've never felt so well and so free as I do right now. I'm very tired though."

"And well you should be, having carried all those secrets for so long. Tell you the truth, I'm tired as well. I think I'll take my covers, add another log to the fire and then go to sleep." Timmy stretched.

"Sounds like a good idea." Tasha yawned. "If you'll remember I was sound asleep before you guys decided to play games in the middle of the night."

All three laughed as they gathered their bedding and prepared for the night. In a short time silence reigned over the little campsite in the midst of the darkened valley.

-28-

Suzy opened her eyes to see a small meal set before her. She was sitting and resting against a boulder. The sun shone directly on her but was very low in the western sky. She drifted back in her memories to another time she had fallen asleep while resting in the warm sun. So much had happened since that day above the circus. She looked up and saw Marlen, Sapphira and a soldier having a small meal. She blushed at the thought of sleeping while the others were busy.

"Ah! It's good to see you're awake. I hope that little nap's refreshed you." Marlen looked up from his lunch, seeing Suzy had awakened. "I moved you off my lap so that you'd be more comfortable. It also allowed me to confer with the rest of the group without disturbing your rest. We had a short mindlink with Oran and Gent, the two Sages who stayed with the armies. They fought a fierce battle with the dark army who came pouring out of the darkness. They suffered many casualties but were able to hold their ground and eventually drive the enemy back. The enemy's resistance crumbled with the dark soldiers fleeing into the desert. We believe the rout took place about the time that you overcame the rogue stone. Gelder, Burgan and Gerold, the other soldier, have already begun their return to help with the healing. We decided to prepare a meal for us before we set off."

Suzy was to her feet immediately. "Let's leave right now. We can't afford to sit around when your help's needed. We must go at once."

Both Marlen and Sapphira smiled at Suzy's response. "A few minutes for eating will be made up quickly by legs filled with energy and determination. You've had a long day and you need the nourishment. We'll get everything else ready." Sapphira pointed to Suzy's plate.

Rolf, the companion soldier, was already up, cleaning his plate, which he returned to his pack. He then took the Sages' empty plates and began cleaning them. Suzy sat down reluctantly on the boulder and began to have the meal that had been set out for her. It certainly was tasty and soon she was glad that she had been required to eat; she felt her strength renewed and her energy increased. She drank some of the soldier beverage and once again enjoyed its refreshing taste. As she finished the last morsel Rolf whisked away her plate and cup to clean it. Suzy decided to walk around a bit to loosen up and to be on her own. She had seen the Sages move off to converse together.

When she returned to the group, she found her pack ready; Rolf helped her strap it in place. Marlen took the lead and the party set off with Sapphira and Rolf following Suzy. They watched as the sun set in the west and the sky turned a crimson hue. They still found it easy to manoeuvre among the rocks since there was sufficient light to travel. They journeyed on without talking as the darkness of evening grew and as the stars began to twinkle to life in the sky above.

Suzy had no idea how long they had marched but she kept up the pace with the rest of the group. She knew they had travelled a fair distance through the darkness but she had no way of knowing how much time had elapsed. The waning moon finally rose casting shadows across their path but allowing faster travel by its dim light.

Sapphira suddenly stopped and so the group stopped moving. She giggled for a moment and then with joy in her voice said, "I just had my first mind thought from my sister in centuries. It's wonderful. She wanted me to know that she's been healed of her sickness and wants to come back to meet the Sage council. I can hardly believe it. She sounded wonderful, positive and free. This is a gift that's unexpected."

Everyone hugged Sapphira, including the reserved Rolf who usually was stiff, formal and disciplined. Suzy was overjoyed for her friend. "How did it happen?"

"Suzy, she didn't tell me. She just wanted me to know. Isn't it wonderful." Sapphira paused for a moment. "Oh! I shouldn't have stopped our return trip. We're needed back as soon as possible. Marlen, you received that latest mind thought from Oran, didn't you?"

Marlen nodded gravely. "Yes I did. It seems that the wounded soldiers are afflicted with some deeper poison. Although none have yet died, it's taking a great deal longer to heal each of the wounds and then combat the poison. We're needed back immediately to help with the situation. I believe we're at least two hours from the battle field so we need to continue our return."

Sapphira spoke softly, "We really need more help but there's none available since the other Sages are back at the Sage Palace and much too far away."

Suzy interrupted her friend, "How far away are Emeralda and Timmy? If they're nearby, they could come to help."

Marlen and Sapphira looked at each other and then nodded their approval of the suggestion. Suzy continued, "Marlen, you once said that if I ever needed Emeralda to come to me, although before this I could never have imagined why, I was to hold that emerald ear stud in the palm of my hand and squeeze it. She'd be obligated to come at once. Isn't that correct?"

Again, Marlen nodded. "Your memory's excellent and your reasoning's sound. Of course, we could try a mindlink but that'd also be open to Natas. I believe your way's better and safer. It's also mandatory for Emeralda – she'll have to come at once."

Suzy reached for the little golden chain around her neck. She removed the chain while holding it in the palm of her right hand. She then closed her hand over it and felt it grow warm to her touch. She also felt a gentle vibration and a slight prickle to her flesh. She opened her hand and returned the chain to its place around her neck. *I think that's been taken care of.*

Marlen looked at Sapphira and then to Suzy. He seemed to be at a loss of what to say. He just shrugged and looked out over the desert. Sapphira spoke instead, "Emeralda's some distance away in the valley of the lodestone. If she really hurries with her companions, it'll take close to a day. That may be too long but it's the best that can be done under these circumstances. In the meantime, we need to be on our way so that we're all able to do whatever we can to help those soldiers to recover."

Suzy shook her head. "I'll be of little help at that. Why not leave me with Rolf; we'll come as quickly as we can. Sapphira and you, Marlen, should go ahead because you can cover the distance much faster than we can. You could be healing soldiers instead of accompanying me."

Marlen wanted to protest but he caught a slight eye signal from Sapphira. He paused a moment to collect his thoughts and to consider what Suzy had just said. "You're right again. We could be back sooner this way and Rolf can protect you.

Of course, if you were with us you'd have more protection. However, this close to the main force should mean you're safe enough to travel with one guard." Marlen paused and stroked his beard. "Still, I'd be more comfortable if we'd take the extra time and travel together."

"I can't allow you to do that, Marlen. I appreciate your concern for me but back there are young soldiers who are suffering and may even be dying. You and Sapphira are needed as soon as you can get there so stop arguing and delaying. Just get going. Rolf and I'll be along. I trust Rolf to protect me."

Sapphira laughed as she saw the puzzled look on Marlen's face. "You need to spend more time with this one, dear friend. You'd learn a great deal about her."

Marlen grinned and then picked up his staff, "Take care, young one." He turned to Rolf, "Watch over her well, good soldier."

Rolf replied with a salute. Marlen turned and headed out into the desert with Sapphira striding at his side. As Suzy had known, they were soon covering great distances with each of their strides.

Rolf and Suzy started on their way following the trail that the two departing friends had made. They soon lost sight of the Sages and settled into a more leisurely pace. The landscape began to lighten as the eastern sky became a lighter pink colour. Walking was much easier now that they could easily see where they were going. Maybe, they relaxed too much because they were surprised to be facing three rogues who jumped into their path from behind a pile of large boulders.

The dark intruders were grinning from ear to ear as they looked leeringly at Suzy. "What do we have here, wandering in the desert with only one armed guard. It looks like the princess that the dark lord wants captured and brought to him.

You'll be priceless to us. Save yourself from any danger or injury by simply surrendering. We won't harm you. Natas wants you in prime shape." The three laughed as they fanned out to surround the two travellers.

Rolf drew his sword and produced a knife from his leg sheath. Suzy dropped behind him drawing her short broad sword and slipped her arm into the shield she was carrying. She took a position back to back with Rolf to protect his backside. Before the dark soldiers had time to arm, Rolf threw his knife at one of the soldiers who sank to his knees with the knife buried in his left shoulder. The two remaining soldiers were now facing an enemy on even terms; they were wary of the outcome.

Rolf waited and Suzy knew that the attack would come her way since she was the weaker and more inexperienced fighter. Rolf spoke quietly so only Suzy would hear him, "When I give the signal step to your left and turn outward. We will do this twice and I'll take on your opponent. If we do it smoothly we'll catch them by surprise and use it to our advantage."

The soldier facing Suzy leered at her, "What are you doing with that sword, little girl? You're only going to get hurt. But if that is what you want, here have it."

Rolf said, "Now."

Suzy performed the required moves in quick succession and suddenly the attacking enemy found himself face to face with a veteran soldier who engaged him quickly. The enemy dropped back and the other soldier moved against Suzy. Rolf again called out the signal and again the two rotated to face the opposite opponent. It worked again.

The enemy soldier facing Suzy said to his fellow. "We must both advance if we're to be successful."

"That's all well and good for you," his fellow fighter retorted.

"Do it now, you coward."

Suzy knew they weren't rotating this time. She gritted herself for the onslaught. The enemy came in swinging his sword, which she deflected with her shield. Her opponent had been so confident of his attack that he left his left side open. She slashed out at once and opened a long gash along the length of his left arm. The wound began to gush blood as he screamed and stumbled to his knees clutching his wound. The remaining fighter dropped back as Rolf pressed his attack. Rolf reached down to pull out another knife. The enemy had had enough. He turned and fled among the boulders and soon was out of sight.

Rolf turned to check on Suzy who had dropped her shield, kicked aside the fallen soldiers' swords and was setting aside her own blade. As Rolf stood guard, she drew a scarf-like garment from her pack that she tore lengthwise to form three bandages. She applied one to the soldier's upper arm and tightened it cutting off the blood flow to the wound. He had lost some blood but not as much as it had first appeared. She then wrapped the second strip around the lower arm closing the wound. She left the top bandage in place as she turned to the first soldier who had gone down.

The knife appeared to have missed any large blood vessel but remained firmly in place. It had pierced through the flesh and had been stopped by the blade bone at the back. It had to come out before the wound could be attended to. Rolf moved over and pulled it out as she applied a chunk of her garment to the opening to stop the bleeding. She took the terrified soldier's hand and placed in on the patch pressing against the wound. "Hold this in place firmly. I'll wrap you up to hold this pad in place once the bleeding stops. You need to help." He nodded.

Suzy returned to the first soldier. She released the top bandage to allow blood back into the lower arm. Rolf was busy tearing a sleeping sheet into strips. Suzy took some of these and added wrapping to the arm and then tied the arm in a sling-like position. She urged the soldier to sit down against a boulder to rest and to prevent any further bleeding. She turned her attention to the second soldier and soon, with Rolf's aid, had wrapped him around the shoulder and chest. He too was placed against the boulder with his friend while Suzy dug through her rations. She pulled out some trail mix, which she offered to the wounded pair. They hungrily wolfed down the food and had a long drink. They smiled their thanks

Suzy and Rolf cleaned their weapons and tossed the enemies' blades behind a boulder. Rolf scouted around the immediate area but could not find any sign of the third intruder. He returned and helped Suzy gather everything together in preparation for resuming their march.

Suzy turned to the wounded men. "We can't leave you here in your condition. You must get to your feet and come with us. It won't be comfortable but you'll manage provided we leave now and walk at a pace that you can handle."

They looked at her and then at the veteran soldier standing over them. They knew they didn't have any choice. Moreover, they were grateful for the assistance they had received from such an unlikely source. They had never heard or experienced such treatment from an enemy. They knew from their background that you either killed the wounded or left them to die. They clamoured to their feet and set off following the young girl who had helped them. Rolf brought up the rear with his hand on his sword. They were surprised to discover they had renewed strength and their wounds did not hurt as severely as they'd expected.

They found the journey back much easier as they followed the trail that was clearly before them since the sun had risen on a new day. As they walked over a rise, they saw the battlefield spread out before them. They descended quickly into the camp to be met by soldiers who placed the wounded behind a detention fence with the other prisoners.

Suzy accompanied them within the enclosure and checked their wrappings. They seemed okay. "You don't need an immediate healing. You can wait until the Sages have taken care of the more serious wounds."

She left this area and went to find Sapphira. Her friend immediately sent her to help the wounded whom had not yet been treated by the Sages. She busied herself bringing food, drink, and making the wounded comfortable. She soon found herself so occupied that she forgot about all else.

-29-

Mera roused Timmy and Tasha from their sleep before sunrise. "Quickly, friends, we must be up and on our way as soon as possible."

The two young people climbed out of their sleeping clothes to find that the sky was still dark and the moon was high in the sky. The night air had a slight chill to it. The fire had burned down to coals. Timmy considered throwing on some logs but Mera had said they needed to hurry. They rolled up their sleeping clothes and assembled their packs as Mera set out some rations for breakfast. Once their packs were together, they had some water to drink and ate the food cold. They then wandered away from the camp on their own to prepare for the journey. After washing up by the stream and filling their canteens they met back at the campfire which Mera had already extinguished. All that remained were hissing embers and a plume of steam rising in the cool air.

Mera brought them close. "I need to explain. I'm sorry to rush you but I received a calling from something to which I'm greatly attached and bound to follow. I've also had a mind thought from Sapphira who asks us to hurry; Timmy and I are needed for the healing of many wounded soldiers after a battle with the dark forces. We've a long march ahead of us, so we must on our way at once. The sun will soon be rising, probably about the time that we leave the valley."

"Well then, let's get going. If the two of you are needed, we can't be standing around here now, can we?" Tasha said soberly.

They walked away from the stone shed at once without any further comments. Travelling was slower; it was still dark and the land was full of rises and dips. They continued to climb higher in the direction they had entered the valley. The sky in the east had a definite lighter shade indicating that a new day was soon to break. The path was now steeper and made its way through a tree-lined trail. Mera came to a stop, looking ahead carefully. Something was lying on the path. The young people approached with their hands ready on their weapons. Mera bent over the mound on the path and grunted.

Mera turned to the other two. "It looks like one of your captors, Tasha. He appears to have been killed in a skirmish. See, he has his sword in his hand and it's stained with blood. He obviously wounded his attacker but fell in the battle. Look, there on the grass and fallen leaves - there's a trail of blood. I don't think his opponent went very far. Let's move on to see where he ended up."

As Mera had suggested it was only a short distance to the next body, which also lay on the path. He had dropped his sword a few steps before collapsing. A large upper body wound was caked with blood indicating death had come quickly.

The sun was now just coming over the horizon behind them; the new daylight reflected off a bright disk on the dead man's tunic. Emeralda looked at it for a moment and sighed. "Well, that's a relief. These two didn't get out of the valley to tell Natas about its whereabouts. It looks like they quarrelled about something and ended up killing each other."

Tasha stared at the disk on the dead man. "Maybe this one realized the other had lost his disk and that led to a confrontation. Whatever happened neither lived to tell about it."

Timmy looked up at Mera. "What do we do with them? Do we leave them or do we take the time to bury their remains?"

Mera looked about and shook her head. "I wish we didn't have this delay. We're needed at the battlefield. However, we can't leave these bodies exposed to the weather and wild predators. We have to bury them. A short distance back there was a rock and gravel outcropping. If we move these bodies to the base of the slope perhaps we can get enough material to slide down and bury them."

"That's probably the easiest and the quickest. We don't have tools with us to dig a grave. Let's try that idea, Mera." Timmy looked back the way they had come.

"Should we be leaving that disk behind? Will it not lead Natas into this valley?" Tasha looked at the disk on the man's shirt.

"Oh! That is a problem. We can't leave it and I can't take it and neither can Tasha since she already has one in her possession. Two could be very dangerous." Mera shook her head,

"I guess that leaves me to carry it," Timmy suggested rather hesitantly

"No. You can't do that, Timmy. When you tried to pick up the first one you experienced a terrible pain. You must not try again with this one."

"But Tasha, what choice is there?"

"I'll take both of them out of here. I'll separate them as we travel and I won't carry this one until we're about to move. If that proves to be too much to do, I'll let you try, Timmy, but not before." Tasha gave Timmy a stern look.

Mera shook her head in disbelief at the courage and determination displayed by this young woman. Tasha doesn't belong here. She wouldn't be here except I tricked her. Yet, she's willing to be involved in a dangerous mission. The more I watch her the more I'm convinced she has a key role to play in the events of this world. What other choice do we have? None, I'm afraid.

Timmy nodded; Tasha reached down and removed the disk from the tunic. She noticed a loose thread at one of the tunic's seams - very carefully, she worked it free. She then used it to fashion a rough necklace for the disk that she did not place around her neck but hung over a tree branch. She turned to see that Mera and Timmy had picked up the body and were carrying it down the path. Tasha bent down and picked up the sword that was lying on the ground. She observed that it was a rough, crude instrument, not at all showing the craftsmanship of the one she carried. Tasha carried it down to the second body where she retrieved that sword as well. She transported this cargo down the path to the base of the gravel slope. Here, Timmy and Mera laid out the body of the first soldier.

"Take those swords up this ridge to those two rocks higher up near the gravel ridge." Mera pointed to the top of the steep rise. "Timmy and I'll fetch the other body."

Tasha climbed over the rugged and uneven ridge of rock. It was hard work climbing while carrying two swords and all packs. She had to be careful that she didn't slip. She reached the two rocks and turned to look down the slope. Timmy and Mera were placing the second soldier beside his fallen companion. *What an odd irony. They killed each other and now they'll be buried together.*

Tasha watched Mera and Timmy climbing the ridge; they moved much quicker that she had. Shortly, all three were busy prying at the large rocks to loosen them. Mera worked on one and was able to dislodge it from the clay so it began to roll down the slope. As it did, the gravel dislodged and cascaded down the slope, sweeping over the bodies. Timmy and Tasha succeeded in prying loose their rock causing a large sheet of gravel to slide downward followed by a large cloud of dust. A more than adequate covering for the corpses resulted from these efforts. The three made their way down the ridge and back up the path, pausing only for Tasha to pick up the second disk which she placed in her other pocket.

They continued up the hill and out of the valley. At this point Mera turned north off the path they had used in arriving in this location. She paused a moment and looked off in the distance. "That delay will mean that we'll be unable to walk to the battlefield until dusk or after dark."

Timmy came up beside her. "You could just tell us the way and then go on your own. I know that you can morph into a bird and cover the distance much faster."

Mera laughed. "A bird, dear friend. How kind you are! You should have said a crow for an old hag like me."

Timmy shook his head disapprovingly. "Don't be putting yourself down again."

"You know, Timmy, that's one of your most endearing traits. You're always concerned about how others view themselves. You're gracious, always trying to be helpful. I'm not complaining, mind you; you've done so very much for me."

"Isn't that the truth." Tasha added. "I'm happy you're here with me, Timmy. You've looked out for me all this time even when I must've been a burden."

Timmy looked down at his feet as he blushed. He didn't know what to say as his friends laughed at his response. Emeralda said, "See, that's what I mean. Yes, I could go on my own but that would mean leaving the two of you and that's something I've promised not to do. Remember! I said I'd stay with you until you were back home. However, there may be another way, if you're up to it, and I mean up to it. I hesitate a little because there are some risks but we do have a lot of ground to cover without much delay."

"Well, what is it?" Tasha asked at once.

"I do have the ability to change my form into that of a bird but I can also change others into that form as well, if they're willing."

"Then let's do it. I'm willing to go ahead and try it. However, I can't speak for Tasha."

"In a sense you already have, Timmy. I can't hold the two of you back and I'd be dreadful on my own. I'm not sure about this changing, especially into a bird that flies, but I won't hold you back. Sure, I'll give it a try."

"Well, not so fast. We'll have to leave much of our gear here to reduce our weight. We can always return for it later or send someone to pick it up." Mera pointed at the slope. "I see a small depression in the hillside below that boulder. We can put our stuff out of sight. We'll add a cover of branches to conceal it the best we can for now. I suggest we take a quick drink and a bite to eat."

Mera paused and looked at her friends. "Even, if you don't feel like it. After that, I'll transform one of you and give you a little training. Just don't try any brave or sudden maneuvers; I know you'll be just fine. Stay close to me at all times."

Tasha and Timmy sat down and pulled some rations and water from their packs. Mera indicated her thanks but said she didn't need any. She then said that she needed something from her pack and disappeared behind a clump of trees.

-30-

After a several minutes during which the two young people finished their snack she returned, having exchanged her black dress for a beautiful deep green gown. She handed her pack to Timmy who with Tasha sat spellbound by the gorgeous woman before them.

Timmy shook himself free of his trance. "Leave your packs with me; I'll put them in the depression and cover them over. In the meantime, Tasha, you go with Mera for the first lesson. I'll be along shortly for mine."

Mera and Tasha walked into a clearing; Mera explained what Tasha could expect. "Although your body will change it won't be permanent - you will remain completely rational and in full control of all your thinking processes."

Mera explained how to lift off, use the air currents to move without expending large quantities of energy and pointed out how to lose altitude slowly to come to a safe landing.

Suddenly, Mera changed into a large hawk and with a few flaps of her wings she was aloft, slowly circling overhead. Tasha felt a sudden shift and realized that she too had changed. She tried a flap and rose slightly, only to come back down on her feet. She then took complete control, flapped her wings several times and rose into the air. Tasha set her wings into a gliding pattern and floated in a circle over the clearing. She caught sight of Mera flapping and did likewise, rising above the treetops and higher into the air.

Tasha then heard Mera say. “Let’s land.” She set her wings to slow down and found herself rapidly descending. She adjusted, flapped once and stopped her descent. She again set her wings and this time glided to the ground landing a few feet from Mera who had resumed her human form. Tasha felt another shift and found herself standing beside a beaming Mera.

“Wow!”

“You were great, Tasha.”

“A couple of moments but nothing frightening.”

Timmy came up beside them. He was smiling as he looked at his friends. “Great job, Tasha! A beautiful set of birds.” He grinned mischievously.

Mera laughed. “I’m so glad to be back as a hawk again. I was becoming tired of being a cackling, old crow. It’s been a long time since a young man called me a beautiful bird.”

They all laughed and then Mera proceeded to repeat the same instructions she had given to Tasha. Soon all three of them were airborne and flying over the clearing. Again, she repeated the rise and then called out for a landing. Both Mera and Tasha landed after a quick descent. They watched as Timmy circled around and as he tentatively made his first landing. He came in a little too fast and had to rise again to drop in a second time. As he landed, he toppled over for a moment much to the amusement of his companions. He picked himself up and in his human form laughed at their jibes. Mera explained that they wouldn’t practise anymore but would head off for their destination. She cautioned that they had to stick together during the flight. They would be flying high enough to avoid arrows and smaller birds that did not appreciate an invasion of their territory.

Soon, the three majestic hawks were winging their way high above the trees and plains heading in a northerly direction. Timmy and Tasha found they could communicate but did not in order to save energy and to concentrate on flying. They were exhilarated by the experience, being able to see for a great distance and being able to see very small animals scurrying through the grass. It was so amazing that they didn't feel any fatigue, even after flying for so long. They passed over the remnants of a castle that had long since collapsed and then over a small villages where the inhabitants looked up as they passed over, shaking their fists to the sky.

Timmy and Tasha wondered what had upset the villagers but soon they were flying over a group of soldiers which, in a straggling line, was marching slowly. Mera took them higher as the men shot arrows towards them. Their keen eyesight allowed them to see that they were soldiers of the dark who had just recently been in battle - many were walking wounded. They could tell that they were covering distance very quickly and as such, the battlefield must not be much farther ahead. Timmy caught a glint of sunlight from below in a grove of trees so he called out to his companions. They circled overhead and discovered an encampment of soldiers who were resting. They did not seem eager to be on their way; in fact, the soldiers seemed to be preparing for some activity,

The three hawks flew on and coming over a rise in the land, they spotted the battlefield. They could see that many people were moving about, carrying wounded enemy soldiers to wagons and leaving the corpses where they had fallen. Timmy and Tasha could see people in coloured robes in one section of the camp going from one bed to the next. They spotted an enclosure in which enemy soldiers sat or lay despondently. Weapons remained strewn over the entire battlefield - all able and available hands were being used to pick up the wounded and to attend to their injuries. They floated down into the middle of an unoccupied area and landed, shifting forms just after touch down.

Suzy looked up from the soldier she was attending to see Timmy, Emeralda and a girl walking across the battlefield. She gave a short wave and immediately went back to the care she was giving. She was happy to see help arrive and especially to see her close friend safe and present.

Timmy was surprised to see Suzy in the midst of all the turmoil but he didn't have time to ask questions. Without any instructions, Emeralda and Timmy joined the other Sages who were tending to the wounded. No one spoke: each knew what to do as quickly as possible.

Timmy found himself immersed in work; he performed healings which were like they had been before, except that as the final measure of healing for each soldier took place he felt a deep chill and a burning sensation in his legs – the same pain he had felt as the black mist had swirled about him when he had healed Emeralda. After a few healings, he simply closed his mind to the pain knowing that it would be there for each healing that he performed - except that it wasn't. He didn't feel the pain whenever he healed an enemy soldier; only the healings of soldiers of the light produced the painful effect.

Timmy moved on to the next soldier who was covered in dried and caked blood. He was barely breathing. Suddenly, Timmy recognized the man before him as his good friend - the commander of the forces, Blog. "Suzy, Tasha, come quickly." He called out and immediately placed his hand on the feverish brow of his friend. Suzy gasped on seeing the injured Blog.

Timmy looked up. “Wash him up and clean out those wounds with warm water. We need to help him as quickly as possible. He’s very near death.”

Tasha hurried off and returned with a bucket of warm water and clean cloths. The girls began to bathe the wounded man and Tasha brushed his forehead. She sighed deeply, rose and walked over to the water supply. She picked up a canteen of cold drinking water and returned to Blog. Tasha took a clean cloth, dampened it and wiped his brow and forehead. He moaned slightly.

Suzy continued to clean the wounds. *This girl’s a great help. I wonder who she…, of course, she’s the decoy Emeralda used to trap Timmy. She’s very pretty and that red hair’s gorgeous. Hmmm, Timmy’s been with her for quite some time….* Suzy laughed, as she realized what she was doing. Tasha stared at her with a bewildered look while Timmy didn’t respond.

Timmy felt himself sinking into a deep, deep hole as he worked at healing Blog. He found an opening in the wall and entered it. A long hallway stood before him and again as he walked down its length the doors opened. Light burst into the corridor from each of the rooms and once again, he found himself facing the final closed door, which refused to budge. He reached for his bracelet, unlocked the door, and braced for the pain he knew was coming. The pain was intense as a green mist swirled out of the room and around him.

A voice screamed at him, “Why do you torment me so? Can’t you just go away and leave my own to me? Do you have to interfere in everything I do?”

“Be gone, you old devil.” Pain shot through him as Timmy lifted his hand from Blog’s head.

Blog was breathing quietly and his temperature had dropped. Timmy got up and moved on to the next soldier.

Rolf came up with some soldier drink for everyone. Timmy immediately felt refreshed and found that his task was much easier than before, although the pain from Blog's healing persisted.

-31-

Many of the wounded soldiers, once healed, ate a meal and regained their strength. They walked out to the battlefield to gather the enemy dead into a large pile. They began to cover the lower surface with soil as more bodies were added to the stack. Increasingly, more soldiers were becoming busy with that task and with the cleaning of the battlefield. The Sages wound up the healing of their soldiers and proceeded on to the enemy. These were straightforward and soon they were even caring for the imprisoned.

Suzy looked up and saw a wonderful sight. Sapphira and Emeralda had crossed the camp and were embracing as long lost sisters. Everyone stood back as they watched this astonishing reunion; many fought back tears. No one had dreamed that such a meeting would ever take place.

After a short time, Sapphira waved to her young friends to come forward to join the sisters. Suzy found herself staring at the beautiful woman dressed in green. It was Emeralda but not the witch who had caused her grief for so long.

Timmy came up and spun Suzy around. "So we finally meet again in Gorn. It's good to see you." Suzy grinned and looked deeply into Timmy's eyes but didn't say anything before Timmy continued talking.

"Suzy, this is Tasha who at first I thought was you. I was really mistaken there; she's really remarkable in that she thinks things through before acting." He laughed - Suzy poked him in the ribs. Timmy jumped back from Suzy. "Tasha, this is Suzy."

Tasha flashed a smile at these two friends. "What a wonderful guy he is, Suzy. If I thought I had a chance I'd steal him from you." Timmy and Suzy both blushed at her words but smiled at each other.

Tasha turned to Sapphira. "Hi, I'm Tasha, a friend of Mera. I'm the one she brought into Gorn to help rescue the lodestone, with the help of Timmy here, of course. You must be this fine woman's twin sister which, of course, is very obvious."

Sapphira broke into a laugh. "I thought only Suzy could be so straightforward as to be called blunt. However, I now see that I was wrong. Maybe, all young girls from your home are this outspoken." Everyone broke into laughter.

Sapphira waited for the laughter to stop. "Yes, I am Sapphira and I'm the twin sister to this beautiful woman. Mera, you said. She hasn't been called that since we were young women so long ago and then only by her sisters. It was our term of endearment for her; already, you're using that name. That's too good to be true." Sapphira had tears trickling down her face.

Mera stepped up and hugged her sister. "I too feel the same way." Tears were running down her face and soon everyone was weeping with joy.

Sapphira regained her composure. "As I said, you're already calling my dear sister, Mera. That's just wonderful. It's so good to hear."

Suzy looked up and shouted with happiness as she spotted Blog striding across the field towards their group with Marlen following close behind. Suzy ran forward and stood still as Blog saluted her. Instead of returning the salute, she stepped forward and Blog grabbed her by the waist and spun her around. Then he set her down and hugged her. When he let her go, he turned and hugged Timmy who had come up beside them. He then stepped back, saluted Timmy, and dropped to one knee as Suzy frowned.

"Thank you, dear prince, for healing me of my injuries, even a deep and hidden wound from long ago. I owe you my life once again."

Timmy stepped forward, took Blog by the hand, and drew him to his feet. "I acknowledge your gratitude and I'm happy that you're healed but, dear Blog, don't kneel before me, your friend."

Suzy smiled as Blog turned to her with a look of bewilderment. Suzy shrugged her shoulders. "Told you so."

The commander walked with his friends back to greet the Sages and the other young woman. Mera turned to Marlen. "I've so much to say to you, old friend, if I can be so bold as to call you that. First, I must say how sorry I am for all the names I've called you or used in reference to you over the years. I'm grateful to this young man who didn't spare himself but stepped forward to heal me. Now, he suffers consequences as a result of that noble deed. However, before we talk anymore, I must tell you that over that ridge is a camp of dark soldiers preparing for action. I believe they're counting on the coming evening in order to launch a surprise attack."

Blog stepped forward at this news. "If you'll excuse me, I'll go at once to organize a reconnaissance party to capture this group. If we move now we can catch them unawares and the battle may be short." He stepped back, saluted and turned, striding away quickly with purpose in his step.

Timmy turned to the group. "I'll go with him. He needs to know about the other group of soldiers who are fleeing from this place so we can stop them before they reach the village that lies in their path. They're in desperate need of food and care; most will perish before they get very far. In fact, the locals may come out to kill them. I'll go along to help with the injured and the sick." He turned and walked after the commander.

"Emeralda, your help was very welcome and very unexpected, to say the least. You've been a major obstacle for us and, in fact, only two nights ago we knew you were near the lodestone, diverting our attention and concentration when it was needed elsewhere. We couldn't send anyone either to prevent you or to rescue you should you try to take possession of that stone. We knew you'd been injured so it's now both a surprise and a relief to see that you've recovered." Marlen spoke in a flat tone to Emeralda.

"Yes indeed, I was injured, Marlen. I did give in to my inner desire to hold the stone once again, forgetting the consequences of the earlier episode. Thank goodness for these fine young people who've healed me of that injury and also of the remnants of the very first encounter with which I've suffered since."

"You say you've been cured of whatever afflicted you earlier but how can that be. I remember we Sages tried to rid you of all injury after your first encounter with the lodestone. We obviously didn't succeed and now you want me to believe that you're completely healed. As much as I hope that's true, I must admit that I'm skeptical about your claim. How do we know whether you're not playing with us to win us over so that you can go back to your ways of trying to recapture the stone?" Marlen shook his head, displaying his doubt.

The group stood for a few moments in silence. Mera let her head hang in acknowledgement and shame while Sapphira looked off in the distance as if trying to be elsewhere. Suzy fidgeted, not certain of what to do. Tasha, however, turned a deep shade of red as she tapped her foot on the ground.

"Sir, I've not been introduced to you yet. I'm Tasha and for the past few days, I've been a companion of Mera. True, I started out as a prisoner and was only supposed to be a lure. However, Timmy and I gained our freedom. Since then, we three have worked together. I wish Timmy had stayed to clear up this mess but he's needed elsewhere. I've only known Mera for a few days but in those few days, I've seen a new person emerge from deep darkness. Do I know if it's genuine? I held her in my arms twice as Timmy reached deep inside her to rid her of all that ailed her. I sat with a pathetic bag of bones resting in my lap and saw her come together as a beautiful Sage. She then walked away from the lodestone that had enticed her for so long. I heard her voice change. I saw her actions change. The second time she underwent healing was after suffering a deep and terrible nightmare. Timmy asked her if she was willing to open all the doors and she agreed. She did struggle for a short time but she managed to overcome the temptation. Mera let all her hidden secrets go. At that precise moment, she became caring and concerned for everyone. She wanted us to be with her and she helped us travel as quickly as we could, as majestic hawks. Does this sound like the old Emeralda?"

"Well, well, well," Marlen said, slightly taken aback by Tasha's impassioned defense of Mera. "Obviously, something's happened to Emeralda if even you can bear witness on her behalf. I apologize for not introducing myself earlier, my dear Tasha. I am Marlen, the head of the council of Sages. You must understand that while I really want everything that I've been told about Emeralda to be true I must, for the safety and security of all of Gorn, be very cautious. I thank you for your testimony because you have more reason than most to really despise her. Emeralda's done much harm to you yet you speak up for her."

"Of course, I do because I've seen what has happened. I wish Timmy were here. Can you hold off judgment until after he returns? Oh yes, there's one more thing; we no longer call her by that name. We use Mera instead."

"So I've noticed. That's another sign that something remarkable has happened."

Suzy spoke up. "Marlen, do you remember that Sapphira said her sister had contacted her? That hadn't happened for a very long time. Surely, that says something. The speed with which she heeded the summons should also mean something. What about the great help she was in healing those injured in the battle. Does this seem like the Emeralda of old? In fact, I do have something that belongs to you, Emeralda. You came at once and now I think you should have it."

Suzy reached for the little gold chain on which hung the emerald stud. She held it out towards Emeralda. This action surprised Marlen and he frowned that Suzy had made the emerald stud visible. However, before he could voice any opposition, Mera stared at the treasure and shook her head. "You'd return that stud to me? Oh, how many times I've searched for it but couldn't go near your home. No, I don't deserve to have it back at this time. I want you to keep it safe, dear princess. Please call me Mera as your friends do. I don't wish to hear that wretched name again." Mera spoke in a whisper.

"Well, that convinces me," Marlen said. I've seen and heard enough to have my doubts erased, dear Mera. I was quite harsh but I hope you see that it was necessary. Put the stud away, Suzy. It shouldn't be seen by anyone outside this group." Marlen turned to Tasha. "Mera, you've developed quite a loyal friend in this one." Tasha smiled in response.

"Quite undeservedly," Mera murmured. "She, of all people, should hate me. I can only be amazed and grateful for all the care that these two young people have given me. Now I'm offered my emerald stud for which I've searched such a long time. What a fool I've been for so long. I want to be part of this great work and I can only hope that all of you will support me as I distance myself from my past."

Sapphira hugged her sister. "I'll always be here for you, dear sister, and you know the rest of the family will feel the same way. The council has grieved your loss since the injury you suffered. We tried hard to restore your health but one room remained locked and unavailable to us. As it turns out, that chamber held the secret to your problems. How Timmy was able to open is amazing."

"Not really that amazing," Timmy said as he approached the group. "I had a great deal of help from Mera who allowed me to go that deep. The key to the room hung around my neck. Our enemy's not very original. His seal is the same no matter where one finds it and it's false. This bracelet's a perfect match and allows me to open whatever he tries to lock away. The room was filled with a blackness." Timmy paused as he shuddered at the memory of the pain caused as that darkness had swept out of the room. "The room's now clean and whatever was there no longer bothers Mera. I also found the same lock within Blog."

"Yes, the darkness has been removed physically but our memories retain copies of it. Mera will have a struggle as time passes because we remember and relive our pasts; sometimes we try to recreate them, to repeat them. We'll be there whenever you need us, dear friend," Marlen said encouragingly. "Speaking of Blog, I thought you were going with him."

"Yes, we leave at once but he asked that Suzy accompany him. He has so many questions for her," Timmy replied.

"Dear Blog." Suzy laughed. "He really has become interested in knowing more about being saved."

"Well, he asked that you, Tasha, and Marlen accompany us on this adventure. He says that each of you have special gifts to share."

Suzy beamed and Tasha looked somewhat puzzled at this request. Timmy continued, "Tasha, you've such a wonderful and gentle touch around injured people. You're a great nurse – everybody you helped has commented on the care you provided."

Tasha blushed and remained silent. Timmy led the group away towards the waiting army, leaving the sisters, one in green and one in blue, standing together in the midst of the battlefield.

-32-

The mop-up operation proved to be less difficult than first expected. Blog's army was able to surround the enemy camp completely without detection - the sentries were battle-tired and nonchalant about their duties. When the camp realized that they were surrounded most of the soldiers had cried for surrender. There had been a short time of unrest and uncertainty when the commander and his officers ordered everyone to fight but the majority of the soldiers refused, disarming their commanders. Then the camp laid down their arms; a closed-in area was built to detain the prisoners. Marlen and Timmy healed the wounded in the camp, much to the surprise of the captive soldiers. Soon, they were asking what this meant that even they, the enemy, received care. They were amazed that the young people came to see them providing nourishment and talking to them. All of this was new.

The second part of the operation, which everyone assumed would be the easier, ended up being more problematic. The fleeing enemy group had already pillaged some farms; those victims were in hot pursuit. Blog's soldiers had the task of dealing with a group of desperate, hungry and wounded soldiers and a force of revenge-seeking victims who wanted justice served according to their demands and wishes. As part of the veteran army held off the farmers, the rest were winning over the enemy in the same way they had done previously - kind words and gentle actions proved to be stronger than threats and the use of force.

Marlen talked to the farmers who felt deeply wronged having suffered the loss of property and dignity. He gathered the leaders together to discuss a new way of solving this problem. He allowed the farmers to air their frustrations and losses, after which he asked what they really wanted. For the most part, the farmers wanted a restoration of what they had worked so hard to achieve. Very few wanted blood and vengeance: through careful negotiations, an agreement was reached: the Sages, the Sage army and the enemy prisoners would rebuild the pillaged farms. Once the farmers reached this agreement with Marlen, they quickly withdrew, returning to their burned out farmsteads to find their families. The soldiers quickly marched the prisoners back to the base camp by the battlefield.

Over the two months that followed, the soldiers and the prisoners went about the tasks of rebuilding the countryside. The locals came to trust the soldiers who didn't behave at all like the dark fighters. New roads and bridges were built; commerce began to occur between the villages of the region. During that time Mera, Tasha, Suzy and Timmy travelled overland to the valley of the lodestone to retrieve their hidden goods. They didn't venture into the valley but proceeded on to the camp where the wagon was still waiting for their return. They found the horse nearby as Mera had said they would. They made their way along the river and enjoyed travelling together, talking about the many different events that had happened. They finally arrived at the palace of the Sages where they were met by the army returning from the east.

Tasha spent her time back at the palace, visiting the libraries and talking to several Sages who filled her in on the history of Gorn and its folklore. She went to see Marlen. "Marlen, I was attacked by two ruffians in the valley while Timmy was looking for Mera."

"These attackers made their way into the valley of the Lodestone. This is serious."

"Timmy and I found these disks. I have two in my pocket." Tasha pulled them out and went to hand them to the Sage.

Marlen frowned and refused to touch the devices. "Communication tools of the dark lord. He uses them to keep track of his followers. You are safe carrying one of them – two could be dangerous, allowing Natas to track your movement."

"Can't we just destroy them?"

"No, that wouldn't be wise. We have no idea how much dark power Natas has stored in each."

"Then someone should take one from me."

"Yes, indeed, someone should, but it can't be anyone from Gorn. They would be in great danger."

"Timmy can't handle either disk. When he tried he suffered pain simply by being close."

"We'll call Suzy. I'm sure she'll carry one."

Suzy was sent for and when she heard Marlen's request she agreed. "I have one question, Marlen."

"What is your question?"

"How long do we have to carry these devices?"

"You'll take them home with you. Once there, bury them in a safe place."

Timmy spent some of his time with Blog discovering what a great leader he was. He also passed a great deal of his time with Marlen who questioned him in depth about his encounter with Emeralda and her recovery. Marlen rubbed his chin and gazed off in the distance. "Timmy, you have done a great thing. However, you will pay a heavy price for interfering with Natas, for stealing away one he thought was his."

"I don't care. I'm happy I was able to help. Look at how alive Mera is."

"Yes, Mera's recovery is wonderful, but you will suffer some of the pain of each victim you heal from now on."

"I know. I have already experienced that discomfort. But I still say it was worth it."

"It could get worse."

Suzy spent time with Sapphira when the Sage was not with her sister, which was seldom, and with her good friend, Blog, who insisted on studying her Bible during every spare moment. She spent hours going over various stories and sharing her many studies. Sometimes, Timmy joined them - Blog was deeply moved with their experiences. Finally, Blog made a decision: he wanted to be baptized.

Before the many residents of the palace, the Sage Council and the assembled army, Blog knelt before Timmy and Suzy as they poured water over his head and pronounced the words they had been taught.

Tasha stood by watching. *I must find out more about this. Timmy, Suzy and now Blog have a special gift that brings them great joy and comfort. I must talk to them about it.*

Timmy and Suzy embraced Blog when he stood up. The army gave him three cheers and a salute. The Sages simply nodded their approval.

Suzy then took her salute from the army; when she turned towards the Sages, she saw a beautiful sight. Four beautiful women stood together, laughing and embracing each other. She immediately recognized Sapphira and Emeralda. *The other two are just as beautiful.* One wore a deep-red dress that complemented her red hair while the other was dressed in a silvery-gray gown that accented her blond hair.

Suzy walked over to the group. Mera stepped forward and gave her a hug. *I have to get used to this. It seems strange to be hugged by Emer… Mera.*

"Suzy, these are my sisters, Ruby and Diamondia. We call them Ru and Mona.

"So! Three of you have special names of endearment. What about my good friend here? Surely, she has a special name?"

Mona laughed. "You mean she hasn't told you we used to call her Sappy."

They all laughed, especially when Sapphira protested loudly. Diamondia continued, "Oh, that's right. I'm wrong about the name. We call her Phira, even now when the three of us… oh I mean, when the four of us get together." The other sisters nodded; Mera wore a special glow at being reunited with her family.

"Phira, that's nice but I'll stick to Sapphira, if you don't mind, dear friend. I've known you by that name for so long that I'd find it difficult to change, especially right now."

Timmy and Tasha were introduced to the group. The three young people walked over to Marlen.

"Well, it's time to go home," Timmy said.

"Yes, my friends, we've enjoyed our adventure together and appreciate all the wonderful gifts you've left us. Mera and Phira will walk with us."

Suzy spoke up as they walked down the road from the Palace. "I do wonder about one thing, my good friend. When I came to Gorn the last time, I used my last portal. What happens now?"

Before Marlen had the chance to reply, Suzy noticed a shimmering directly before her. Marlen chuckled. "You are inquisitive, dear princess. From now on, you'll be able to call up a gateway anytime you wish. When you lost that gem, that valued crystal in your necklace, your reward is this gift. Use it wisely; use it well."

Suzy walked through followed by her companions. They found themselves on the roadway just outside the farm just before sunrise. The three young people said goodbye to each other and set out for home. Marlen accompanied Timmy, Tasha by Mera who would explain her late arrival home to her anxious parents and Suzy by Sapphira. Suzy gave her dear friend in blue a hug, then cut through the trees into the yard quietly entering the house by the back door. She left her backpack and quietly made her way up the stairs to her closed door.

"Suzy, please come into our room, sweetheart," her mother called.

Suzy went into her parents' room. They were both awake and sitting up in bed. Her mother tapped the bed, "Sit down here, sweetheart, please tell us all about your adventure in Gorn. Exactly, how are our dear friends Marlen and Sapphira doing?"